After so many years of contented independence, could Em finally have found love?

"Unless I miss my guess, we'll be seeing Chance before the month's out," Megan announced. The laugh in her voice sounded rich. "Don't you think so, Em?"

Em cast a questioning glance over her shoulder at Megan. Faint moonlight showed only shadows, but Megan caught Em's movement.

"Don't be so innocent, Em. That man's interested in you."

"In me?" Em's expressive voice told that she doubted Megan's sanity. "That's fiddle-faddle!"

"No, it isn't. I saw how he looked at you."

"At my age? A man? You is out o' your mind, Miss Megan."

"Now hold on," Banjo intervened, chuckling. "I've got a mite o' snow in my hair, but I ain't dead yet. Neither are you."

Megan laughed, delighted. "I have a pink dress we could make over for you, Em, if you want."

"Land sakes, child! Let it rest!"

Megan's soft laughter graced the breeze, but she didn't say any more.

ROSEY DOW, resides with her husband and seven children in Grenada, West Indies. Their work in the country is as missionaries. Rosey manages to find time to write about one of her favorite places—Colorado—between sharing the Gospel and home schooling.

Books by Rosey Dow

HEARTSONG PRESENTS
HP204—Megan's Choice

Em's
Only Chance

Rosey Dow

Rebecca Walsh

Heartsong Presents

To my children:
David, Darrell, Miriam, Jonathan,
Nathaniel, Steven, and Jim.
Without you my life would be so empty.

A note from the author:
*I love to hear from my readers! You may correspond with me
by writing:* **Rosey Dow**
Author Relations
PO Box 719
Uhrichsville, OH 44683

ISBN 1-57748-457-6

EM'S ONLY CHANCE

Cover illustration by Lauraine Bush.

PRINTED IN THE U.S.A.

one

Em Littlejohn rushed to the open door of the cabin where shouts of laughter and playful barks drifted in from the Colorado ranch yard. The broiling August sun made her squint and shade her eyes. In spite of the hurry, Em paused for a smile.

Eleven-year-old Jeremy Wescott rolled on the grass in a mock wrestling match with Lobo, the wolf-faced dog his sister had tamed.

"Jeremy! Come in this instant! You'se got to change now or we'se a-gonna be late for the barbecue!"

Lobo nipping at his heels, Jeremy trotted toward the cabin, his face glistening, his strawlike hair standing on end.

"Wash up in the spring out back," she continued. "I'se got your clothes laid out in the loft." The mouth-tingling aroma of freshly baked bread that filled the house touched her senses as she stepped back a pace.

"Is he coming, Em?" Megan Chamberlin, Jeremy's grown-up sister appeared in the doorway of the master bedroom. She smoothed the full skirt over her rounded abdomen. With the baby due in just eight weeks, this outing to the Rocking H would be her last for some months.

In answer to Megan's question, fifty-two inches of boy burst into the room. Pulling at his shirt buttons, he took a curved route past the two-person settee in the living room, around the gingham-covered dining table, and through the kitchen to the back door. His destination lay a wagon-length behind the house at a stone-lined basin where a spring flowed from a crack in the orange rock cliff looming five hundred feet above them.

Jeremy's words came from over his shoulder. "I'll be ready in a jiff, Em." The slam of the back door put a period to Lobo's final bark.

Tall and lean Em wore a new navy dress with gathered skirts and only two petticoats. The ex-slave's brown face had soft lines around the eyes, across the forehead, and beside full lips. Her cheeks had the texture of tissue paper, crumpled then flattened again. Black hair—gray strands woven through it— lay in shiny cornrows straight back from her forehead, ending in a knot at her nape. Tender devotion filled Em's wide-set eyes as she gazed after the boy. Her boy. As much hers as if he were her own flesh. For twenty-two years, Em had showered every ounce of her lavish mother love on the Wescott children, Megan and Jeremy. At the end of Mr. Lincoln's War, the sobbing woman had begged Katie Wescott to let her stay with the family. Megan's widowed mother hugged her childhood playmate, and with tears of her own, Katie pledged that Em would always have a place with them.

Megan joined Em beside the dining table. Navy gingham curtains gently lifted in a soft breeze. "It's hard to believe, isn't it, Em? Fifteen months ago Jeremy could barely sit up. Often I thought that rheumatic fever would take him." She embraced the slim lady beside her. "I could watch him run and play from dawn to dusk just counting my blessings."

A lump tightened Em's throat. "You'se right about that, Miss Megan," she said huskily. "That boy's a seven day's wonder." She shook her head as though to shake off the sentimental mood and eased out of Megan's arms. "I'd best finish hookin' up these shoes. We'se a-gonna be late for sure." Three paces later, Em disappeared into her quarters—a new addition built off the dining area at the west side of the cabin, a narrow room with a plank floor, a cot, and four pegs on the wall.

A solid stone wall at the front and squared logs made up the rest of the Circle C cabin. Directly across from the front door, the master bedroom cut into the open living area, leaving an L-shaped space. The short section jutting toward the back was the kitchen. At the center of the front wall, smooth stones fitted closely together on the gray floor and on the gleaming orange fireplace. Two pegs over the thick mantel held the Henry rifle that dainty Megan Chamberlin could use to outshoot her husband.

The cabin was no bigger than a carriage house in the Old South where the Wescotts had their roots. The open-beamed ceiling over the front half of the cabin gave the impression of space. The floor of the loft—Jeremy's domain—formed a ceiling to the bedroom and kitchen at the back.

Twenty minutes later the buckboard lurched ahead with Joe Calahan—the Circle C's only hand—holding the reins. Known to everyone as Banjo, his innate kindness and good humor had won the hearts of Megan and her husband, Steve. The old cowhand had helped them find Christ last November.

As usual, Jeremy sat between Em and Banjo in front. After Jeremy's and Em's arrival, Banjo had built a second seat on the buckboard. Steve and Megan always sat in back. Banjo called theirs the Lover's Seat.

"Can I hold the reins, Banjo?" Jeremy raised his pleading face toward the grizzled cowpoke.

"Soon's we cross the creek, Jem," came the answer. "You remember the words to "Power in the Blood"? At Jeremy's nod, Banjo led out, his rough voice filling the air, "Would you be free. . . ?"

The buckboard rattled around the tasseled, rustling corn-field, and the house was quickly hidden from view. Heat shimmered down from a merciless sun. A brown grasshopper surprised Em by jumping on her skirt. Grimacing, she quickly flicked it off.

Busily sniffing, feathery tail high, Lobo followed the wagon to the creek bordering the lower edge of the gently sloping field.

"Go home, Lobo!" Steve called, waving at the dog. Ears up, eyes watchful, Lobo stood on the edge of the trickling water, tail softly waving, until the wagon swayed over the creek, up the rutted incline, and out of sight.

Traveling southwest, the little party bounced along a rough trail through rolling hills randomly covered with towering firs and spindly pines. Beside wagon-driver Jeremy, Em let her body roll with the pitching wagon. Was it only twelve weeks since she'd walked garbage-laden streets filled with clanging trolleys, clomping horses, and clamoring newsboys? The stench of animal and human filth had shrouded everything.

Like overflowing buckets, Em's lungs drew up the pine-scented air. Her fingertips tingled. After scratching out a bare existence during the seven tedious years since the war, Em felt reborn. A thousand times, she'd prayed for God to help her suffering family. Now that the blessing had fallen, she could hardly contain it.

When Banjo's song finished, the only sound besides Jeremy's shrill, excited voice was the sweet trill of a mead-owlark. Before them lay a sparkling green and brown world with a wide blue dome for a lid. Fluffy, cotton-wool clouds floated from invisible threads.

Again, Banjo lifted his voice toward heaven. "There is a fountain. . ."

The wagon's right front wheel dropped into a dry puddle. Em gripped the seat and blended her contralto with Banjo's bass.

❧

The Chamberlin party arrived at the Rocking H an hour before supper time. Five times the size of the Circle C, the Rocking H had belonged to Victor Harrington. After he'd been murdered, it had passed to his daughter, Susan, and her husband, Wyatt Hammond. Susan and Wyatt shared the running of the outfit. Married only eight months before, they were more than lovers. Wyatt and Susan were partners.

At the last rise, Rocking H buildings came in view. Banjo said, "Thanks, Jem. I'll take over from here." He retrieved the reins from Jeremy's fists and pulled the wagon to a creaking halt beneath a cottonwood on the edge of the compound.

The Rocking H sprawled before them—a circle of buildings around a center yard. The ranch yard looked like an ant hive today: women with baskets of food, a few men carrying sawhorses and boards to make tables, and others carrying benches. Sizzling beef sent up an odor that made all comers glance at the time, wishing away the minutes until time to dig in.

While happily greeting the guests around her, Susan organized the table quickly filling with baked beans, potatoes of every kind, vegetables, and mountains of biscuits. On the edge of the clearing a black man tended the barbecue pit—a wide hole filled with glowing coals. Two feet above the heat source, a glistening side of beef turned slowly, skewered on a six-foot pole with a handle on one end. This was the source of that heavenly aroma.

Jeremy leaped to the ground the moment Banjo stepped down. He scampered across the grassy yard toward the beef, ready with fifty questions for the cook.

Banjo ambled around the wagon to help Em alight.

"Thank you kindly, Mr. Banjo." Her words had a soft, husky quality that was easy to listen to.

"Now, Em," Banjo playfully chided, "you and I've been gettin' on right fine, but that *mister* stuff has got to go or we'll be fallin' out. Ain't nobody ever mistered me in my life."

She reached into the back of the wagon for the basket full of bread, baked that morning. "Yes, sir," she said, then halted when she saw Banjo's eyebrows raised in mock indignation.

"Yes, what?"

"I mean, yes, Banjo."

"That's better." Banjo's friendly grin summoned a wide smile from Em, showing glistening teeth.

Laughing, Em added, "You is a caution, Banjo. And that's for sure."

During Banjo's bantering with Em, Steve had carefully eased Megan down from the wagon. He placed her hand on his arm and covered it with his own. The foursome strolled toward the low, wide ranch house. Half a dozen men lounged on the broad porch, chewing tobacco and swapping yarns.

Striding shoulder to shoulder, the Rocking H foreman, Curly Hanna, and his boss, Wyatt Hammond, strode toward them, welcoming grins gracing both faces. Wyatt's new tawny beard gave him a jolly appearance. Shorter than long, lean Wyatt, Hanna outweighed his boss by almost sixty pounds. At the edge of his wide hat, bushy eyebrows contained every hair on Curly's bullet-shaped head.

Wyatt tugged the brim of his flat-crowned brown hat as he nodded to Megan. He punched Banjo's shoulder, then grabbed Steve's hand. "Good to see you folks! How's life treatin' you?"

"Couldn't be better." Steve clasped Wyatt's hand. He shook Curly's meaty paw. "How'd the cattle drive go?"

Curly's words came forth strident and loud, the voice of a man used to giving orders. "Great! We lost nary a head, found good grazing all the way, and didn't see hide nor hair of any Injuns. We got back three days ago."

Slim and girlish, her strawberry-blond ponytail gleaming in the late afternoon sun, Susan Hammond arrived ten steps after her husband. She put her arms around Megan. "Megan! How are you? It seems like weeks since we've talked." She glanced at Wyatt, Curly, and Steve jawing with Banjo. "Let's leave the men to talk about their favorite subject and find us a nice seat in the shade." She touched Em's arm. "I'm glad you came, Em." Arm in arm, Susan and Megan strolled to a bench beneath a wide oak.

Behind the younger women, Em took stock of the busy scene before her. The party atmosphere reminded her of another time, another life. She could almost hear the vibrant voice of Megan's young mother, the laughter of elegant guests, the slaves dancing in the moonlight after the white folks had gone to bed. Those days had ended years ago, but they lived in Em's memory as vividly as though it were yesterday.

She sensed the same spirit here. Yet, she also felt a great difference. In Virginia she had been an integral unit of the plantation. Today, among strangers, she was a little afraid. How would these people react to a black woman, a former slave?

Em carried the basket to the food table. Two ladies arrived within seconds of Em. Neither looked at her. She might have been invisible.

Returning to the bench where Megan exchanged the latest

news with Susan, Em's eyes sought out Jeremy. The boy stood before the busy cook, chattering and pointing. Curious, Em observed the dark man turning the spit. She had an urge to walk over to him.

Did he have a family? What had he suffered? How had he come to the Rocking H?

What's wrong with you? she scolded herself. *No one's introduced you to him. You may be more than forty years old, but that don't mean you can rush up to a strange man and ask him his life's story.*

During the next hour, she forced her attention away from the barbecue pit several times.

Suddenly she realized that Mrs. Pleurd—a barrel-shaped woman with quick, birdlike eyes—had stopped to greet Megan. The newcomer glanced at Em, acknowledged Megan's introduction with a noncommittal nod, and turned to Susan. "Are the Feiklins coming?"

"Here they are now!" At Susan's announcement, all eyes turned toward the wagons and carriages amassed on the eastern edge of the yard.

Curious about the newcomers, Em watched their approach with interest. Formerly from Texas, Sheriff Feiklin had brought his family to Juniper Junction only six weeks ago, at the invitation of the town council. Rumors flew among the townsfolk that trouble with his oldest daughter had convinced the lawman to accept a position in a new place.

Led by Sheriff Rod and his wife, Sally, the four members of the Feiklin clan strolled across the clearing. A faint breeze rustled the leaves overhead. An irate jay scolded the rude humans below him.

Thick, wide, and strong, Rod walked in the loose-jointed gait of a man long in the saddle. He carried a hefty front porch that lapped six inches over his belt. His booming voice cut through the hum. "Yes, Mama, Lisa has the basket."

Sally cocked her ear toward him, squinted slightly, and nodded. Eight inches shorter than her husband, Sally had been a beautiful teenager, but time and childbearing had left her stout, with round, dimpled cheeks. Under his Montana-slope Stetson, her husband's hair was thinning and gray, but hers was thick and black, pulled into a fat bun.

Lisa and Jessica paced behind their parents. Nineteen-year-old Lisa, the elder girl, was a buxom lass with flashing black eyes. She stretched her neck, taking a tally of the guests.

Jessica jabbed her with a sharp elbow. "Lisa!" she whispered. "Don't be so shameless!"

"What's the matter, little sister? Afraid I'll catch a fellow's eye before you?" With long slim fingers, she raked through her thick mane, flipping her hand out as she reached the end.

"Lisa!" Jessica's firm mouth twisted in exasperation.

The pair seemed as unlike as two sisters could be. Lisa's curving cheeks softened her square features, and Jessica's high cheekbones gave the impression of flatness to her heart-shaped face. Lisa had flawless, milky skin. Jessica grew a crop of light freckles across her nose, and her cheeks always blushed.

Both girls had wavy hair that matched the color of a raven's wing, but bright sunlight brought out red highlights in Jessica's high chignon. Held back by two tortoiseshell combs, Lisa's mane cascaded to her waist.

"Afternoon, Mrs. Hammond." Rod Feiklin raised his battered hat. "Mrs. Chamberlin."

"This is Em Littlejohn." Megan stretched her hand toward Em. "Last May she and my brother came to join us from Baltimore."

Feiklin gave a short nod without looking directly at Em. His voice raised five decibels. "Sally, I'll leave you to gossip with the ladies."

His wife nodded. "Okay, Rod." Gathering her wide skirts, Sally settled onto the bench beside Susan. She waved at Lisa and Jessica as though shooing chickens. "Take the basket to the eatin' table and enjoy yourselves, girls."

Lisa hitched the basket closer to her waist and sauntered away. Casting a frustrated glance at her mother, Jessica's lagging steps trailed her sister.

Sally flicked open a fan and dove into the conversation. She squeaked like a young mouse. "How do you like Lisa's new dress? It's sprigged muslin. I finished the hem last night." She plowed ahead, hardly drawing a breath. "I tell you, I had the awfulest time with Rod this morning. The moon's waning so I wanted him to help me turn our feather-bed. Lord knows, it's too heavy for me or the girls." She sniffed. "He told me I'm silly and superstitious. I had to put my foot down. . ."

Em soon tired of the conversation and wandered toward the crowd around the table, hoping to lend a hand. She'd be more comfortable working than listening to Sally's prattle. Jeremy ran to meet Em in the center of the yard.

"Want to see the cow gettin' barbecued?" he asked, his brown eyes sparkling. "Chance is the cook. He let me turn the crank for him." He clutched her hand and pulled.

Em chuckled. "I'm coming, Jeremy. You don't have to drag me." Now that the moment for meeting the cook had arrived, she felt a little shy.

two

"Chance, this is Em," Jeremy announced moments later. He might have been introducing the president.

Bent over the bubbling, searing carcass with a dipper of red sauce in his nimble fingers, the cook looked back over his shoulder. He stopped in mid-motion, eyes on Em. Slowly, deliberately, he returned his attention to the beef, poured on the remaining sauce, and straightened to his full height. Orange-red coals hissed as drips fell from the meat.

Though she was above average height, Em's head scarcely reached the bridge of the man's nose.

He ducked his head and said, "Glad to know you, Miss Em. You new in these parts?"

"Yes," Em replied. "I brung Jeremy to the Circle C three months back."

"He's quite a little fella." Chance's expression warmed as he smiled down at Jeremy. With skin the color of coffee mixed with a healthy dose of cream, his high cheekbones made him look almost Hispanic. Deep creases ran down the center of both cheeks and from the corners of his nose to the sides of his mouth. Fixing his gaze on Em, he said abruptly, "You workin' for his family?" He sounded gruff, suspicious.

It wasn't what Em had expected. Her chin rose. "I'm part of his family," she countered, matching stare for stare.

An instant later, Chance relaxed. A grin curved his full, expressive lips. "Where are you from?"

"Virginy." Em glanced at the sauce-smeared bowls set

15

around the pit. "Can I help you with something?"

"Sure enough. In a few minutes I'll cut the meat off the bone. You can slice it into small pieces and carry it to the table." He paused, watching her closely as though trying to make a decision.

"Can I help, too?" Jeremy begged.

Chance chuckled, amused by the boy's anxious face. "Sure can, Jeremy. You hold the handle of the spit, so the meat won't move while I'm cutting it." With deft movements his knife carved out a five-pound roast. Using a long fork and knife as pincers, he placed it on the platter Em held ready, then he reached for another from the stack on a stump nearby.

They worked in silence for twenty minutes, a silence punctuated with soft words like, "Move the handle a little to the right, Jeremy," and "Here's another ready for you, Miss Em."

Em looked up to catch Chance watching her again, that questioning slant to his brow. Her face suddenly grew warm. When the last meat plate lay on the table, people began easing toward the food like cows to the barn at milking time. Two barrels of water stood to one side with a dipper hooked over each rim. Bowls, plates, and pans covered every square inch of the table.

Wyatt and Susan stood together facing thirty guests. Wyatt raised his hand high and conversation died. He stroked his beard self-consciously. "We're mighty glad to have you folks with us today. If you don't get enough to eat, it's your own fault." Gentle laughter rose from the ranks.

He continued, "I suppose it's fittin' that we thank the Good Lord for the food before we dive in. I'm not much of a hand at prayin', so I'll ask Banjo to do the honors."

Hat in hand, Banjo stepped from the ranks, head bowed.

His graying black hair fit close to the scalp, a crease where his hat brim pressed.

Soon afterward Jeremy and Em loaded tin plates and located their family at one of four long tables lined up parallel to the vittles table in the center of the yard. When they arrived, Megan moved closer to Steve to make room for Em. Jeremy scooted in next to his pal, Banjo. As the boy sat down, the light softened. Dusk lurked thirty minutes away.

"Where'd you two get off to?" Megan asked.

"I was helping Chance," Jeremy declared. "He let me turn the barbecue spit."

"Chance?" Megan glanced inquiringly at Em.

"He's the cook," Em replied, keeping her eyes on the beef, biscuits, and beans before her.

"Oh, yes. I know who you mean. I never knew his name before."

"He's real nice," Jeremy continued.

Banjo laid down his fork and grasped a tin cup of water, saying, "He's been here about five years, I reckon. Keeps mostly to himself."

"I like him," Jeremy declared. He picked up an ear of roasted corn and opened his mouth wide.

Rancher Sanders and his Mexican wife, the older Feiklins, and the Hammonds filled the remainder of the table. A few feet away sat Jessica and Lisa with their friend, Elaine Sanders, an olive-skinned beauty with features like a china doll. At the opposite end of the girls' table lounged the Rocking H hands. Various visitors from town occupied the other two tables.

Twilight brought life instead of sleep—clattering forks on tin plates, teasing and hoots of laughter. Fireflies and crickets opened up for business. Darkness brought blessed relief from the day's sweltering temperatures. Mosquitoes came out to enjoy the cool night air. Two lanterns glowed on each table with more lanterns hung from nails on three trees and a post.

Chance had found a seat with the hands. Halfway through the meal, Em winced when a booming voice sliced the pleasant atmosphere.

"Hey, boy! Fetch me some water, will ya?" Holding his tin cup high in Chance's direction, a Rocking H puncher, Jake Savage, was the brawn behind the voice. Every ounce of two hundred twenty-five pounds, Jake looked fat, but his biceps didn't know it. Woolly black hair brushed his shoulders. "I say, boy! I'm talkin' to you!"

At the end of the table, Chance stabbed a morsel of beef and carefully placed it in his mouth. He chewed three times. Slowly facing Savage, his answer came out low and without expression, but the words carried far. "Get it yourself."

"Right, Savage." Curly Hanna spoke louder than Chance had. "Get it yourself."

Silence hung over the party for a count of three. Placing his palms on the table, Savage eased his bulk over the bench and trudged into the night. A sullen scowl twisted his wide, flat face.

Turning to Rod, Mrs. Feiklin asked loudly, "Why did Hanna say, 'Here's to your health'? Was he making a toast?" A relieved titter passed through the ranks. Normal noises returned. Soon afterward Em watched Chance lift his plate and leave the clearing, his bottom lip thrust forward.

Em met his eyes for a fleeting instant as he passed. She expected to see anger, hostility—and certainly, those emotions were present. But mostly she saw sadness. Hopeless sadness like she'd seen in the eyes of Megan's mother as she scratched out a living in the ghetto of Baltimore, leaning over a washboard and hot iron day after thankless day. The impression pierced her through. Shaken, she couldn't eat another bite.

ò&

After the meal, Sanders's pint-sized wrangler named Ernie put his chin on a fiddle and the young folks set up for a square dance. Lisa Feiklin crossed the clearing to latch on to Wyatt's newest hand, Brent Cavenaugh, a blond giant with a baby face and a strawberry mustache. He came willingly, his eyes admiring Lisa and at the same time challenging her. The only flaw to his perfect features was a brown, dime-size birthmark below his right earlobe. Rocking H men—Curly, Slim, and Amos—made up the rest of the form with Jessica, Elaine, and a stout, giggling girl from Juniper.

"Anybody for a man's sport?" Jake Savage bellowed when the music reached full pitch. "I'll take on any comers. Arm wrestling." He sidled onto the nearest bench, elbow resting on the plank table. His fingers looked like sausages, his lower arm like a ham hock.

"Ahm game," responded a muscular hombre sporting a sardonic grin. He sauntered up and claimed the place across from Savage. He had flat cheeks and a wide, flat nose, giving the impression that someone had pushed his face in.

Noting the man's southern drawl, Megan leaned toward Susan sitting beside her. "Who is that?"

"He's the new hostler in Juniper, Link Hensler. He's a good friend of Brent Cavenaugh, Lisa's dance partner." Em watched the contest from her seat at the next table, ten feet from the loud cowhand who'd tried to intimidate Chance. She hoped to see Savage get a set down.

Savage leaned forward to clamp down on Hensler's hand. "Elbows stay down, left hand flat on the table," the big man growled, staring into the hostler's brown eyes. Savage's paw made the other man's hand seem slim as a girl's. Hensler had a jagged bumpy scar on the back of his right hand.

Faces grim, the combatants set to. Hensler's biceps bulged. His ruby red lips stretched tight as sweat rose on his forehead. Savage never changed expression. He coolly regarded his opponent as though he were a steer about to feel the lasso.

A dozen people left off watching the dancers and gathered around Hensler and Savage. Em left her seat to move closer. No one uttered a word.

At first locked hands stayed rigidly still. Soon, straining arms began to quiver. Hensler's yellow teeth showed as he grimaced, fighting to keep his hand up. Savage relentlessly pressed, the hint of a smile on his fat lips.

Quick as a rifle shot, Link's arm slammed to the table. Savage let out a victorious hoot. Hensler jerked his hand away, his breath coming in quick gasps. He wrinkled his nose, sniffing as though he smelled something foul, and strode through the circle of spectators.

Immediately, Kip Morgan, foreman of the Running M, filled Link's seat.

At the edge of the crowd, someone brushed Em's arm. She looked up to see Chance standing beside her, his eyes on Savage.

"He's a thorn in your flesh, ain't he?" she asked softly. The words popped out before she knew. Embarrassed, Em clamped her lips together; she drew a little away from Chance.

As his eyes burned into Savage, the black man's voice grated, low and intense, "He's just like all the rest of 'em. Fifteen years ago, he would have been a foreman with a whip in his hand." Abruptly, Chance about-faced and stepped away. Troubled, Em watched his back until he disappeared around the dancers.

At the table, Savage made short work of Morgan. The first dance over, Brent Cavanaugh and Amos McClintock tested their strength while the girls sashayed with another set of partners.

Brent lasted two minutes.

A Missouri farm boy built like a prize bull, McClintock gave Savage a run for his money.

The grin faded from Jake's greasy face. His shoulders bunched; cording stood out on his neck. Normally ruddy, his face looked like a tomato.

Amos's jaw jutted forward. Their clenched hands eased toward Amos, the farm boy. . .hovered. . .trembled. . . inched toward the top of the arc. Jake pulled in a bellyful of air and held it. Murder gleamed in his black eyes. Amos bent his head toward the table as though in prayer. A desperate battle followed with their hands moving only fractions of an inch. The spectators remained perfectly still; not a breath of noise disturbed the gladiators. Moments passed. The suspense rose to excruciating levels.

Sweat on his forehead and upper lip, Amos strained against Jake's mighty arm. Their arms paused at forty-five degrees.

Savage's arm struck wood.

A collective sigh went up from the group.

Hensler declared, "Weren't that a humdinger!"

Immediately, Amos grasped Savage's hand in a shake. "If you hadn't a-been tuckered out, I'd a been a goner, Jake. Next payday, I'll buy you a sarsparilla."

Reluctantly, Savage nodded, his jaw tight. "Sure, Amos. Sure." He unwound himself from the bench and lumbered into the blackness.

"It's about time we headed out," Steve said, lifting Megan's bonnet from the table and handing it to her. "I'll round up

Jeremy." He lost himself in the gang headed for leftovers on the food table.

Anxiously scanning Megan's tense face, Em asked, "You okay, Miss Megan?"

Megan squeezed Em's arm. "Just tired, Em. I'm fine."

After saying their good-byes, Megan and Em found Banjo waiting for them beside the buckboard. From this distance, the lanterns looked like giant fireflies. As the untiring fiddle belted out a jig, Banjo handed the ladies up and climbed aboard. Jeremy in tow, Steve's tall form split the shadows. Seconds later the wagon lurched ahead.

"Nice party," Banjo offered as they left the clearing.

"It was grand!" Jeremy declared. "When will they have another'n?"

"Not till next year, Jeremy," Em said, slipping her arm around the boy's thin shoulders. Night breezes relaxed taut muscles; the smell of sweet sage soothed their senses. "But we'll be visitin' with Miss Susan and Mr. Wyatt before long."

"How about Chance?" Jeremy asked quickly.

"I suppose so," Em said, softly.

"Unless I miss my guess, we'll be seeing Chance before the month's out," Megan announced. The laugh in her voice sounded rich. "Don't you think so, Em?"

Em cast a questioning glance over her shoulder at Megan. Faint moonlight showed only shadows, but Megan caught Em's movement.

"Don't be so innocent, Em. That man's interested in you."

"In me?" Em's expressive voice told that she doubted Megan's sanity. "That's fiddle-faddle!"

"No, it isn't. I saw how he looked at you."

"At my age? A man? You is out o' your mind, Miss Megan."

"Now hold on," Banjo intervened, chuckling. "I've got a

mite o' snow in my hair, but I ain't dead yet. Neither are you."

Megan laughed, delighted. "I have a pink dress we could make over for you, Em, if you want."

"Land sakes, child! Let it rest!"

Megan's soft laughter graced the breeze, but she didn't say any more.

three

Three days after the party, Banjo slouched on the front steps with his left shoulder leaning against the porch railing. His hands worked nimbly over a hollow stick, whittling.

Em and Jeremy had finished the supper dishes an hour ago. Soon afterward Em, Jeremy, and Banjo had wandered outdoors to enjoy the twilight. Lobo lay, nose on paws, at Jeremy's feet below the steps. Weathered wood grain created a rough texture under the hand Jeremy leaned on.

"Is it almost ready, Banjo?" Jeremy asked, his face inches above Banjo's masterpiece.

Churning butter a few feet away, Em called, "Keep your nose out o' the way, son. You're 'bout to git whittled yourself."

"It's almost done, Jem." Banjo held the whistle toward him and rolled it over in his palm. "I may have it finished by tomorrow night."

"Will you teach me to whittle?" Jeremy's adoring eyes begged along with his words.

" 'Course I will. Next time you go into the woods, find you a chunk o' wood about the size of your fist." His knife moved in regular rhythm, peeling off short, paper-thin strips. He glanced at the boy, a twinkle in his mild blue eyes.

"I bet I can guess how old you are, Jem."

Jeremy straightened to attention. "How?"

"Stand on one foot," the old-timer commanded, pointing to the ground. "Right there."

Still watching the cowpuncher, Jeremy obeyed.

"Now hop around in a circle."

Looking skeptical now, Jeremy again obeyed. Em bit her cheek to keep from laughing. Eyes on his young master, Lobo raised his head, ears tilted forward.

With a serious, calculating expression, Banjo carefully monitored the boy's progress and continued staring at him after he'd finished the task.

Ten seconds later he declared, "You're eleven."

Jeremy scrambled up the stairs and dropped into his former seat, his face alive with curiosity. "How did you tell, Banjo?"

Thick hands sent another sliver of wood to the floor. "Miss Megan told me." He guffawed at the boy's I-can't-believe-you-did-that expression. Em's hearty laughter joined with Jeremy's.

A faint yellow light appeared in the open door. Megan had lit a lamp.

Steve called from inside the cabin, "Jeremy, come in now. It's time to wash up. Bedtime."

"Coming, Steve," Jeremy answered, still smiling at Banjo's trick. He brushed off the seat of his pants and trotted inside.

"That boy fair worships you, Banjo," Em remarked. The handle of the churn made squish-thunk noises with regular rhythm.

"He reminds me of my own," Banjo murmured, turning the wooden cylinder in his gnarled hands. "Funnin' with Jem helps ease the empty place Todd left."

"I never knowed you had a son."

Banjo blew a wood chip from the whistle and placed the toy in the chest pocket of his overalls. He slid the knife into a sheath at his side. Of their own accord his eyes sought the mountain ridge where the orange sun sleepily nestled, but he looked far beyond boulders and sky and earth. His mind stared into another day, another life.

Em felt a story coming on.

He pushed up the front brim of his battered John B. Stetson until the hat rested on the back of his head. "I was twenty-six when I married an angel with hair the color of anthracite coal and a laugh that would charm the birds down from the trees. A year later God gave us a son. He had my eyes and his mother's smile.

"We owned a little spread near the Red River, ran a few cows and worked a garden. Much like Steve and Megan. My boy follered me everywhere, asking questions, anxious to help me in any little way he could." He paused. For a full minute he sat perfectly still. Drawing in a long breath, he went on.

"Back in '58, I left the ranch for two days to pick up a new bull, a big feller to strengthen my herd. When I got home the ranch was nothin' but a heap of ashes. They killed Mary and took my boy, Em. Kiowas." His eyes glistened. Blinking, he coughed. "I wanted to die, too, but somehow I kept on breathin'.

"I sold the ranch and rode the grub line for nigh on ten years—mining here and there, hirin' on as a hand when the notion took me. In '63 I took up with Sheridan. To tell the truth, I still didn't give a hang if I lived or died. Fightin' for the Confed'racy seemed the best way to hang up my saddle.

"Spring of '64 my outfit camped in Mississippi. A young preacher rode out to give us a sermon. Most all of us went to hear him. There wasn't much else to do and with the Pearly Gates loomin' up in front of us every day, we was ready to hear somethin' from the Good Book. After one o' them meetin's I went up and talked to the feller. I knew Mary was in heaven and I wasn't going there." Banjo glanced at Em, a keen edge to his look.

"I made peace with God that night, Em. Jesus is the only reason I can roll out in the morning. To this day I don't know if Todd's alive or dead. I don't even know which would be best. The thought of him livin' off white men's scourings on one of them filthy reservations. . .it's hard to take sometimes." His words faded away. Only the thumping churn handle broke the silence.

Em paused to wipe weary hands on her apron. She smiled, a knowing light in her eyes. When she spoke, Banjo looked toward her, surprised.

"I met Jesus when I'se a child, Banjo. At the Littlejohn house, us house slaves went to church with the white folks. Most o' the people there didn't pay us much mind, like as if we was part of the furniture or somethin'. But sometimes, a little old maiden lady with hair like combed cotton would take us children outside to teach us Bible verses and little songs. Miss Ida her name was." Em's face crinkled as she smiled. "I thought she was an angel come straight down from heaven. I loved her almost as much as I loved Miss Katie Littlejohn, Megan's mama, who was just about my age and my very best friend.

"Miss Ida was the one who told me about Jesus. Me and Miss Katie took Jesus on the same day after one of Miss Ida's classes." She shoved the churn handle down with energy. "One thing I regret, though. I don't know much Bible. I know some gospel slave songs, but precious little more than Miss Ida's verses.

"When Miss Katie married Master Wescott, I went to live with them. We never went to church 'cept maybe to camp meetin' now'n agin. Master Wescott wasn't a believer."

Unaware that he was interrupting, Steve appeared in the open doorway. "Like to play me a game of checkers before turning in, Banjo?"

Banjo chuckled. "Does a chicken have lips?" He got to his feet and raised his hands for a stretch.

Em looked up, puzzled. "Chickens don't have lips!" she said.

He grinned at her. "Why, Em. You've been a city slicker too long. Check 'em out next time you feed them."

Steve shook his head. "If you believe that one, Em, he'll be sure to tell you another one tomorrow." Laughing, the men ambled inside.

Em pounded the thickening butter, lost in sweet memories, oblivious to hoofbeats and Lobo's bark announcing a rider. A tall bay gelding cantered into the yard. Startled, she looked up and recognized Chance astride the saddle. Instead of the white shirt and black pants he'd worn when cooking, he filled out a pair of scuffed jeans and a faded blue shirt. He prodded his mount close to the porch and pulled the flat-crowned black hat from his head. Lobo stretched out his nose for a wary sniff at the horse.

"Evenin', Miss Em." His words were friendly, yet hesitant.

On the porch, Em stood almost at eye level with the caller. She found her tongue at last. "Steve and Banjo are inside. The door's open. You'se welcome to go right on in."

"I didn't come to see the men. . . I came to see you." At Em's bland expression, he hurried on. "That is, I was wonderin' if I could call on you sometime." He slid his fingers around the brim of his hat, around and around, but his eyes stayed steadily on Em. The last rays of the fading sun made his skin gleam like bronze.

Shock numbed Em's brain. "I reckon it won't hurt anything," she faltered. "Anytime."

Chance smiled, showing gleaming teeth. "I have free time two Saturday afternoons each month and all Sundays. I'll be seein' you." He bowed from the waist, his curls falling over his brow almost to his eyes. Moments later, his horse's hoofbeats melted on the breeze.

Jeremy bounded through the door wearing a white knee-length nightshirt. His face glowed from scrubbing, his hair damp around the edges. "Who was that, Em?"

"Chance," Em stated briskly. She grasped the handle of the butter churn and squee-lunked it down. "He just stopped to swap howdies." Jeremy studied her a moment, chirped, "Night, Em," and skipped back inside.

☙

Frantic labor filled almost every waking moment of the next two weeks. Twice the size of last year's plot, the garden yielded bushels of beans, tomatoes, cabbage, carrots, potatoes, and turnips. Every member of the household went to bed with groaning muscles and a wearied mind. Megan tired quickly, so she took the lighter jobs like snapping beans or slicing cabbage.

Late in the afternoon on the thirtieth day of August, Em hurried outside to take the last of the washing from the line while biscuits baked for supper. A thick stew bubbled on the stove. Steve and Banjo looked like miniature cutouts in the garden plot down by the stream, hoeing and pulling out dry tomato plants.

Arms heavy with laundry, Em heard the faint drumming of hoofbeats. She stopped, straining her ears. Suddenly she wondered, *Is today Saturday?* A startled question on her face, she scurried for the house. Lobo, thinking it a game, barked after her.

Inside, she raced to her room to drop the clothes on the

narrow bed and lean toward the window. A tall bay with a white blaze and one stocking bounded into the clearing. Em reached her bedroom door in five strides and spoke to Megan, who sat slicing cucumbers at the table.

"Miss Megan, someone's here. I'll be out in a minute." With that she flipped the door shut and pulled at the fastenings on the front of her dress. She grabbed a fresh dress from a wall peg and dragged it on. Dabbing at her hair with a brush, she muttered, "Em, ya knows you'se too old for this kind of foolishness. People your age shouldn't get so het up over a simple little visit. Fiddle-faddle, that's what it is."

A gentle tap on her door set Em's heart skipping faster. Drawing in a slow breath, she tiptoed over to open the wooden barrier a narrow crack.

Megan's sparkling eyes appeared around the edge of the door frame. "You've got company, Em," she whispered.

Em's face burned. A retort for Megan's teasing look sprang to her tongue, but Em held it in for fear Chance would overhear. Megan stepped away, and Em pushed the door open.

Chance stood in the living room, holding his hat by the brim. He had the look of a law student appearing for his first interview.

"Good afternoon, Miss Em," he said. "I was wondering if you'd like to walk out with me." He cleared his throat. "That is, if you're not busy."

"I suppose I could." She looked at Megan, as though asking for help.

Jeremy pushed through the back door, a basin of freshly scrubbed cucumbers in his hands. He set the basin on the table and glanced from Em to Chance and back to Em.

"Go ahead, Em," Megan urged. "You need a break. It won't hurt me to finish the pickles."

Chance opened the door, and they stepped outside. At the porch steps, Chance laid his hat under the railing. "I'll leave this here," he said. "There's a breeze and I won't be able to enjoy it with my head covered."

Flat wispy clouds reclined on a wide cobalt couch. Above their ethereal brothers, fat white puffs glided past. The northern sky had a darker cast. Shading his eyes, Chance stared at the horizon. "We'll have rain tonight," he predicted. "Lord knows, we sure do need it."

The couple strolled along the flat stretch in front of the stable, the corral—where four horses, Banjo's donkey, and Bess, the Jersey cow, milled about—on past the chicken yard and the bronze-colored cliff that acted as a backdrop to the Circle C homestead. Ahead of them, the ground sloped down to a winding stream that wove through a stand of pines.

"Been working hard?" Chance asked after a lengthy pause.

"Today we'se a-doing pickles. Yesterday we canned a hundred quarts of string beans." Em heard herself talking as though from afar. A camp robber jay bounded for the sky, its beak full of pilfered corn, leftovers of the chickens. Em's skirt brushed a clump of baby blue eyes. The tiny flowers bobbed in her wake.

She felt like a schoolgirl being courted for the first time, futilely trying to keep up her part of the conversation without giving away her nervousness. She hadn't stepped out with a man for twenty-five years.

Across the nearly dry creek bed, Chance leaned his back against a waist-high boulder. "How long have you been with Chamberlins?"

Em perched on a low, flat rock before replying, "In a way I been with them all my life. I'se born on Ebenezer Littlejohn's plantation. He was Miss Megan's grandfather. My mama was a field slave. She died in childbirth. Louisa Littlejohn, the master's wife, came to the quarters when my mama died. She took a shine to me and decided to bring me up by hand in the house. Miss Louisa had a girl two years older than me. That was Katie, Miss Megan's mama. Katie and I grew up together like sisters.

"When I got fourteen, Miss Louisa made me a housemaid. Later, Miss Katie married and I went to be her housekeeper. The war left poor Katie a widow. She had no home, no income, and two children to raise, but she let me stay when I begged to. She could have turned me out, but she didn't. She died two years ago. A few months later, Miss Megan came here with Mr. Steve. Miss Megan sent for me and Jeremy three months ago."

A movement caught her eye. "Look!" Pointing, she whispered, "An antelope with a young'un." The mother flipped her tail and bound into the trees, a baby at her heels.

Man and woman set off walking again. Spindly trees cast long, spiky shadows around them, and an aspen whispered a secret song.

Uncomfortable with silence, Em asked, "How long have you been with Hammonds?"

"A little over five years. After freedom came, I stayed one winter in Mississippi and came nigh to starvation. Every freed slave I knew almost starved that year. The next year I worked odd jobs tending gardens and digging ditches. No black man could get a decent job. Before the war, the poor whites were fairly friendly. Afterwards, they saw us as a threat. They thought we'd steal away their jobs. The third year, I couldn't stand any more, so I started hiking west."

They moseyed south across scrubby hillsides, winding around trees and brush until they reached a three-acre lake surrounded by thick spruce. Em knew this place from her walks with Jeremy. She loved the tranquil atmosphere in the quiet minutes shortly before dark.

Chance looked over the water with a knowing eye. "This place looks like a good fishing hole." He smiled. "I haven't been fishing since Georgia. I used to keep the plantation in carp and panfish. Sitting on the bank of a lake was the only way to get some peace in those days."

"Hammonds seem like good folks," Em commented as they paused at the still water's edge. The lake mirrored the trees, the hawk wheeling overhead, the clouds. Faint ree-beeps wafted from the other side.

"Hammonds are decent people," Chance confirmed. "Miss Susan's daddy, Victor Harrington, was tough as an old corn cob. Once he threw a plate of stew out the door because he got a piece of gristly meat." He chuckled, a mellow, musical sound. "I had to stay on my toes with him around." He swatted a gnat. "But Hammonds are easy to please. Miss Susan's a jewel." Picking up a fat, round stone, he lofted it high, and watched it plop. High circular ripples fanned from the spot. A dragonfly swooped lower to investigate.

Em found a fallen log to lean on. She said, "You know, you talk awful good. Almost like one of them city fellers."

Though the corners of his mouth turned up, bitterness gave the smile a bite. "I had a privileged upbringing. My mama was a housemaid." He bent over to pick up a twig. "My father was the master. I grew up in the house and had a white playmate like you. His name was Gregory. My half brother." He paused, his jaw muscle working in and out. He snapped the twig and threw it down.

"Gregory was as good as his father was wicked. We'd sneak outside with his schoolbooks and run down by the river so he could teach me his lessons from that day's school. It didn't matter to him that he was breaking the law by teaching a black boy to read." He snorted. "A black boy."

He glared at the ground. "Before my fifth birthday I didn't know people took me as being black. I knew Master Collins was my daddy. I lived in his house." He snatched a long blade of grass. "I wasn't allowed in the main part of the house, but I never wondered why. That was just how things were. One day, I sneaked into the dining room and Cook caught me. She grabbed me by the ear and hollered, 'Next time I catch you in heah I'll warm your black hide!' " Chance's slim fingers split the grass and tore strips from it. "That night I asked my mama. I didn't believe it. . .but it was true."

"They treat you good?" Em asked. She couldn't keep her eyes from his sad face. In spite of wrinkles and signs of age, Chance was a handsome man.

"Two months after I turned twelve the foreman tied me up and took me to market. Like a hog. . .or a chicken. My mama screamed and cried. She begged Master Collins to let me stay. My daddy never looked at her or me. He got in his fine carriage and drove away.

"I never saw my mama again. She's probably dead by now. It's been thirty years. After the war I went back to Master Collins's place, but it was burnt, everyone gone. There's no way I could find her, Em. If she died, they sewed her in a canvas sack and dumped her in an unmarked grave. If she's living, where did she go?"

Though she'd heard this kind of story before, Chance's tale jolted Em. Her tender heart dreaded the rest of it, yet somehow she felt compelled to know. "Who bought you?" she asked.

"A small outfit in Mississippi by the name of Pettigrew. They only had a dozen slaves. Master Collins kept more than a hundred. While I was with my mama, I never saw a beating. They did happen once in a while but not out in public. Pettigrew beat somebody almost every week.

"I started out tending the garden and helping the cook. I was only twelve, remember? Because I'm light skinned, they wanted me in the house. Ten years later, the cook had a stroke. I got his job."

"How long were you with Pettigrew?"

"Thirty-three miserable years. I cooked for twenty-three of them. The rest of the slaves got rest days—Sundays, a week at Christmas, and a week for the Fourth of July—but kitchen slaves had to work year around. People always have to eat."

With a parting glance at the water, they drifted back to the creek and along its edge to the wagon crossing. Six inches of water trickled around the mossy stones lining its bottom.

Em glanced at the lavender sky. "It's gettin' on to dark."

"Let's cross here," Chance said, pointing to three flat rocks. "We can step on those." He took two strides, balanced, and turned around to help Em, offering her his hand. As they approached the house, he asked, "What's your name?"

"Em."

"I mean your whole name. Emily?"

"Emma," she replied. "Emma Littlejohn."

"My mama named me Chance. Why, I don't know. I guess my last name should rightly be Collins, but I've never taken it. I'm just Chance." They paused beside the porch steps. He smiled into Em's eyes. "I've enjoyed the afternoon, Emma. Would you mind if I call again?"

Em heard herself say, "I'd be pleasured." At the same second she thought, *You must be teched, Em. It's twenty-five years too late for these kind of goings-on.*

Chance scooped his hat from the porch and flipped it on. Fine white powder puffed around his head. It drifted over his face and hair to his shoulders. Coughing violently, he flung the black felt away. It tumbled to the ground in a cloud.

Em stared, horrified.

Chance brushed powder from his eyes and nose, punctuating the coughs with two sneezes. "What is this?" he croaked angrily. Creases appeared over his eyelids and around his mouth.

Em gasped. "What on earth happened?"

"Somebody put flour in my hat!"

Em covered her mouth to hide a smile.

"What are you laughing at?" he demanded.

"You look like a gingerbread man." Em chuckled. "Sugar frosting and all."

Chance's anger cooled as quickly as it had appeared. He grinned dubiously and reached in his back pocket for a handkerchief.

"I shouldn't have laughed," Em said, still smiling. "I'm awful sorry."

"You look sorry." He wiped his face and bent over to ruffle his fingers through his hair. A white cloud appeared for the second time.

"I'll find out who's responsible, Chance. I'm awful sorry."

"Don't keep apologizing. It's okay." He retrieved his hat, tapped the crown to shake out any loose particles, then pressed it on his head.

"Do you still want to come back?" Em asked, sobering.

"Of course. I'll see you in two weeks." With a nod and tug at his brim, he marched soldier-style to his horse, pulled out the picket pin, and stepped into leather—a futile effort to regain his dignity. A thoughtful, sweet curve to her lips, Em watched him trot around the meadow, a faint white mist surrounding him.

four

Megan stood at the sink, stacking soiled pans when Em arrived. On the counter beside her stood twenty-eight gleaming jars of dill pickles. An iron stewpot bubbled on the stove, sending up a luscious beefy aroma. Jeremy laid wide shallow bowls around the table. He looked up as Em entered.

"What happened, Em?" Megan asked the moment Em stepped into the kitchen.

"We walked to the lake," Em murmured, her mind preoccupied. She picked up the apron lying over the back of a dining room chair and slipped it on. "Chance had a hard life, Miss Megan. He's a sad man."

Sensing Em's sober mood, Megan plunged a kettle into soapy water and didn't press her for more details. Jeremy sent her short, inquiring glances throughout the meal. He seemed restive and unusually quiet, but the adults didn't notice.

Far into the night, Em tossed on her bed. Chance's story played through her mind again and again. What must it be like to cherish only a few spare memories of happiness in a life of almost half a century? She thought about her own past, crowded with people who loved her. Slavery hadn't meant cruelty and rejection to Em. She'd felt little difference after freedom. Chains of love had bound her to the Wescott family tighter than slavery ever could.

What had Chance known of love?

Embarrassed and unsure of her feelings, Em didn't want to discuss Chance with Megan yet. She kept her thoughts to herself until the following day, when she met Banjo in the chicken yard.

After breakfast, Em threw cracked corn to the chickens milling about her feet. In the yard, Lobo clenched a short stick between his jaws.

Jeremy lunged for it. "Give it here, Lobo!"

Gripping hard, the dog backed away, shaking his head to loosen the boy's grasp. Jeremy laughed, captured the bit of stick, and tossed it far across the meadow. Lobo raced after it.

Banjo nailed a loose board on the chicken house, finishing with three hard whacks of the hammer. He fed the hammer handle through a thong on his pants and trudged over to Em. His heavy boots grated on the sandy ground. Removing his hat, he swiped a faded blue sleeve across his face. He adjusted the Stetson to its usual place, friendly eyes on Em.

"What's up?" he asked in his direct way. "You've been actin' like you're on your way to a funeral. When you don't scold me for eatin' five pancakes, something's wrong. Anything I can do?"

Em gazed at him an instant before chuckling. The creases around her eyes deepened. "I don't know if anybody can help me," she replied, shaking her head. "I don't rightly know what's wrong with me." She shook the last of the feed to the clucking, scratching hens. "Chance came a-callin' on Saturday."

"I heard about that," he said. "You like him?"

"I'm too old for this fiddle-faddle," she burst out.

"Now, Em." His tone was similar to that used by parents and schoolteachers. "We've been over that territory before." He repeated, "Do you like him?"

Em watched Jeremy and the dog chasing across the grass. She turned back to Banjo. "He's a fine man on most counts.

But there's a hard core to him that worries me. I can't rest easy in my mind about him."

"Does he know the Lord?"

She shook her head. A dimple deepened on her right cheek—the one Megan called her worry mark. She brushed corn dust from her apron.

"He's mad at God." She sighed. "Likin' Chance ain't the issue, is it, Banjo? He don't know the Lord and that puts a high wall between us." She tapped the empty feed pail against her leg. "I'm awful sorry for him, though."

"I'll be prayin' for you," Banjo promised. He let his eyes follow the romping dog and boy for a long moment.

"There's somethin' else, too," Em went on. She told him about the flour-in-the-hat incident. "I'm afraid Jeremy did it," she finished. "I don't want to tell Megan. She'd be awful crabbed. Her time's so close I don't want to make her fret." She shook her head. "I can't imagine why he'd do such a thing!"

"Should I talk to him?" Banjo asked. "We get along right well. I may be able to help."

"That's a temptin' offer, but I reckon I should be the one to do it," Em decided. She grunted, then laughed in a self-condemning way. "Not that it'll do any good. I can't bring myself to whup the boy no matter what he does. And he knows it. My scoldin' gets to him like rain on a duck's back." Mouth pulled down into a puzzled frown, she headed toward the house.

Banjo's face held a serious expression until Em disappeared through the door. When the door banged, his natural twinkle surfaced along with an amused grin. He muttered, "But I certainly can imagine why Jeremy would do such a thing." Picking up the shovel where it stood propped against the stable, he strode inside to clean out the stalls.

≥∂

Em still hadn't resolved the Jeremy issue the following Friday.

Although September was only ten days old, Steve and Banjo smelled autumn while they saddled up by murky lantern light before dawn. Later that morning, Megan—tired and uncomfortable—installed herself on the settee's tan-and-navy jacquard upholstery to embroider a tiny gown. Em booted Jeremy outdoors to romp with Lobo awhile before the family attacked a basket of late tomatoes for canning.

Em was examining the pantry and deciding on a lunch menu when Jeremy burst into the living room.

"A rider's comin'," he shouted. "I can't tell who it is."

Em met the boy at the door and looked out over his head. "It's a brown horse with black legs and a black tail. You know anyone rides a horse like that, Miss Megan?" She peered through the distance. "It appears to be a small man with a tan hat and a red plaid shirt."

Megan laughed. "That's not a man. That's Susan." She held the baby gown to her face and bit off the short embroidery thread. "Put the kettle on for tea, please, Em."

"I'll help her with the horse," Jeremy declared as the chestnut reached the yard. He strode across the grass in true cowboy fashion and stretched for the bridle far above him.

Watching him through the window, Megan smiled. Jeremy's restored health still brought her delight. She grasped the settee's cloth-covered arm, pushed herself to a standing position, and waddled to the door.

Pulling off her gloves and Boss Stetson, Susan tripped up the steps. She looked exactly as she had more than a year ago on her first visit to the Chamberlin home—thick strawberry-blond mane pulled back into a ponytail, light freckles across a pixie nose. Marriage hadn't changed her one whit.

"Susan!" Megan stretched out for a hug. "How nice to see you!"

Susan's tinkling laugh brightened the atmosphere. "I felt stifled at the ranch today. The men are on the range, Chance is out of sorts, and I felt a mood coming on. So, I threw a saddle on Reggie and headed over here." She lifted her hat to a peg and set her gloves on the shelf above. "How are you, Megan?" Scanning Megan's puffy cheeks and tired eyes, she added, "Don't answer that. I can see you're worn out." Concern clouded her eyes. "Maybe I shouldn't have come."

"Nonsense!" Taking her arm, Megan drew her to a chair. "Sit down and rest your bones. Em will have tea ready in a moment, and later we'll have lunch." Megan resumed her place on the sofa. "Lately, my days are forty hours long. A body can only sleep so much. I'm glad you're here to make part of today fly by." She picked up the whalebone needle and a strand of blue thread.

"What are you making?" Susan asked.

Megan held up the pale blue gown, its yoke half covered with a spidery design in navy. "Another gown. This is the last one. I've got to stop playing and get to practical things, like diapers and bibs. I've got a bolt of gauze for the diapers, but so far I haven't made one."

Em appeared with a wooden tray. She set it on the small table beside Megan. "Good morning, Miss Susan," she said, her dark face beaming. "I sure is glad you decided to call. Miss Megan had a bad case of the blues this morning. You'll pull her out of it for sure." She handed Susan a cup of black tea.

"Why don't you sit with us awhile, Em?" Megan asked,

accepting a steaming cup. "You're wearing yourself out while I sit here like a big. . .like a big. . ."

Em shook her finger at Megan like she was a naughty child. "Don't say it, Miss Megan. You'se doing the best work possible just now. After the baby comes, you'll be plenty busy, believe me." Em fetched a third cup, filled it, and found a seat next to Megan.

"The barbecue went off wonderfully, Susan," Megan said. "We had a marvelous time. Jeremy wants to do it again right away." She sipped tea. "You've hired four new hands. I've never met them before."

Susan's expression tightened. "I don't know how long they'll be with us. Last month we hired two: Brent Cavenaugh and Amos McClintock. A third man, Link Hensler, is always hanging around our place at night and on Sundays visiting Brent and Amos. He's the southern man who first took Jack Savage's challenge in the arm wrestling contest. Hensler's not one of ours, but he's around our place so much some folks think he's on the payroll. Wyatt calls Cavenaugh, McClintock, and Hensler the three musketeers.

"Hensler is the new hostler in Juniper. No one seems to know anything about him. I have a bad feeling about him. About the others, too. They go on a drinking binge every time they set foot in town. Once Brent Cavenaugh asked Wyatt for an advance on his next month's pay. He'd gambled away his whole month's wages the very first day."

She shivered. "Brent's handsome in a saloon kind of way, but he's too vain for my taste. Wyatt says Brent's the only man he ever knew that could strut sitting down." She shivered. "Something about him gives me the willies."

Megan set her cup into its saucer. "Lisa Feiklin doesn't seem to agree."

Em's lips firmed together. "That gal's headed for trouble, Miss Megan. I can tell it just lookin' at her."

"There's another new man besides those three, isn't there?" Megan asked. "The big man who started the arm-wrestling contest?"

Susan nodded. "Jack Savage. He came six weeks before Brent and Amos. He's a hard worker, one of the best we've ever had." She paused, glancing at Em. "But he's got the nature of a loco longhorn. He constantly bullies poor Chance. It gets me riled enough to give him his walking papers. I wanted to, but Wyatt said we need him till winter."

Em froze when she heard Chance's name. *Does Miss Susan know about Chance and me?*

If she did, Susan didn't show it. She went on, "Chance now, he's the best cook we've ever had. He looks for recipes in *Harper's Weekly* like he was a hotel chef. He makes some of those fancy fixin's, too."

Em clattered her cup to the tray and stood up. "It's nice to see you, Miss Susan, but I'd best call Jeremy and get started on them tomatoes. I'll set out some sandwiches in a little while."

Susan and Megan watched Em's thin back until she disappeared into the kitchen. Susan raised shapely eyebrows and looked a question at Megan as the back door banged.

Megan chuckled. "Did you know that Chance has been calling on Em?"

Susan's eyes widened. "No!" She leaned forward, speaking lower, her eyes dancing. "How long has this been going on?"

"Since the barbecue. Em hasn't said much to me, but she's been awful quiet, almost moody. They went for a long walk two weeks ago, didn't come back till almost dark." She ran her finger around the edge of her teacup. "What do you know about him, Susan? I'm a little anxious. Em's old enough to be my mother, I know, but I'd sure hate to see her wounded by a fellow with a smooth line and no scruples."

"You're describing Brent Cavenaugh, not Chance," Susan stated. "Chance is everything a house servant could be, Megan—honest, smart, not afraid to go the extra mile to make sure things are done right. Unfortunately, I don't know much more than that. He never talks about anything but the task at hand. He's polite but reserved in a way that keeps everyone at a distance.

"On his day off he rides out. No one knows where he goes. He doesn't go into Juniper and gamble, that's for sure." She reached forward to pat Megan's hand. "Don't worry, Megan. I think Chance is all right."

"I hope so." Megan's words held a thread of doubt.

Susan stayed an hour beyond lunch. After she rode off, Megan lay down for a much-needed nap. Half an hour later, window-rattling thunder awakened her.

Jeremy darted into the bedroom to hide his head in Megan's shoulder. She patted his hair. "Don't worry, Jeremy. The storm will pass in a few minutes."

"We never had thunder like this in Baltimore." The boy's muffled voice spoke close to her ear. Another crash split the air. The boy jerked, then snuggled closer.

"The storm is God's way of letting us know He's still there."

Em stepped inside the room, her worry mark showing. "I hope Miss Susan made it home okay. She's been gone less than an hour."

"She was raised here, Em," Megan replied. "If she gets caught in the rain, she'll know where to find shelter." She scooted over on the four-poster bed to make more room for Jeremy beside her.

"Jeremy bothering you, Miss Megan? You need to rest."

Megan patted the skinny shoulder next to hers. "Not at all, Em. Before long he'll be too big to want comfort from me. Let him stay."

"I'll fix hot chili soup for supper. Banjo and Mr. Steve are out there, too. They'll be soaked to the hide."

The storm raged through the night. Thick dark clouds scuttled across the sky Saturday morning. As the shadows began to lengthen, Em wore out the floor pacing in front of the front windows. Suddenly, she realized what she was doing and rebuked herself for acting like a lovesick teenager.

Uneasy and vaguely worried, Em sat up late knitting a tiny sweater. Chance had told her he'd come. Why hadn't he kept his word?

Sunday dawned clear and cool. Em stirred the oatmeal and turned bacon in the frying pan while Jeremy helped Megan set the table. On the sofa, Steve studied the family's only Bible, preparing for the worship time he'd lead after breakfast.

A galloping rider shattered their routine and drew everyone to the porch. Banjo stepped from the stable, pitchfork in hand. Whoever the rider was, he had a reason to hurry.

The visitor swung from the saddle and, holding the reins, approached the house. Em recognized Slim Reilly, six foot four and built on the same lines as a pencil. This morning his thin, hatchet face bore marks of deep strain. His high-pitched voice puffed out in gasps. "Wyatt sent me to fetch Mrs. Chamberlin. Susan got soaked in Friday's storm. She took sick yesterday. This morning she's out of her head with fever. Amos rode to Juniper for Doc Leatherwood, but we need a woman to look after her, too."

Em received an unspoken message from Steve's lined brow

and wise eyes. She reached a firm hand out to Megan. "Let me go, Miss Megan," she murmured. "You can manage here, but you're not up to nursin' anyone just now."

Megan nodded, regret tightening her lips. "I suppose you're right." She looked up at Steve. "I do wish I could go."

"It's good of you to offer, Em," Steve replied, slipping a protective arm about his wife's waist. "Banjo, will you hitch the buckboard and carry Em over?" He turned to Slim. "She'll be there shortly."

"Much obliged, Chamberlin." The cowhand took two steps away. "I'll cool off my horse a mite before I start back."

Jeremy skipped down the steps. "I'll do that for you," he offered hopefully.

"Come in for a bite of breakfast," Steve added. "The womenfolk were about to put it on the table."

Fifteen minutes later, Em sat beside Banjo on the front seat of the buckboard. Biscuit-and-bacon sandwiches lay wrapped in a cloth on her lap, a fresh dress in the carpet bag at her feet.

Megan came to the door to wave as the wagon passed the house. "Take good care of her, Em."

"Don't fret yourself, Miss Megan," Em called. "She's in the hands o' the Good Lord."

Leading Slim's horse around the grassy yard, Jeremy looked after the buckboard with intent eyes.

five

A hundred thousand acres of mountains, lakes, and forest surrounded Hammond's spread. The hub of the outfit lay twenty miles southwest of Juniper. From the final ridge, Banjo and Em could see that the buildings formed a ring—the sprawling house, the smokehouse, the corral, two twenty-horse stables side by side lying directly opposite Susan and Wyatt's home. The bunkhouse, a small blacksmith shop, and a tiny grove of oaks completed the circle.

Wyatt strode across the yard to meet them the moment the buckboard came to a halt. He had aged twenty years in twenty hours. His shoulders stooped, the flesh on his face had melted until cheekbones jutted harshly against the pallid skin above his beard.

Banjo helped Em climb down before turning to meet the desperate husband with the words on everyone's lips: "How is she?"

"The same," came the tortured answer. Wyatt stretched a bony, calloused hand to the dark lady standing shoulder to shoulder with Banjo. "Thanks for coming, Em."

"Miss Megan's gettin' too close to her time to come, Mr. Wyatt," Em said. "She wanted real bad to come herself."

"Chamberlin said to tell you they're prayin'," Banjo added.

They moved toward the house. "Doc Leatherwood hasn't come yet," Wyatt said. Shading his eyes, he strained to see as far down the trail as the mountain allowed. "No sign of him yet." Dropping his hand in a despairing gesture, he said,

"Susan's sleeping now. Chance is with her. I didn't sleep nary a wink all night, and I had to get some air."

They stepped across the plank floor of the veranda and into the entry hall. Em glanced around as they moved through the living room and into the master bedroom.

Though not elaborate in any sense, the house had been built with skill and care. A mixture of lime and mud chinked the log walls. The boards in the wide plank floor were of varying widths, fitted together with expert precision. The living room was furnished with cowhide furniture and an Indian rug. Coal oil lamps adorned two small tables and the mantelshelf above a broad stone fireplace. On the right wall stood three doors.

The master bedroom lay behind the last door at the back corner of the house. Two-thirds the size of the large living room, it had wide windows on two sides. Ornately carved fronts adorned the chifforobe, chest of drawers, and mirrored dresser.

Em's attention immediately centered on the massive bed piled high with quilts. The prickly smell of sickness and the grating sound of shallow, raspy breathing gripped Em.

Susan's lips parted as she fought for air. Her beautiful hair lay matted against a ghostly pale face. Beside her, in a rocking chair, Chance got to his feet the moment Wyatt and Em entered the room. Banjo had stopped to wait in the living room.

Chance smiled when he caught sight of Em. "Mornin', Emma." He looked down at the patient, pity pinching his mouth. "She hasn't moved since you left, Mr. Wyatt."

Em moved around the bed and leaned over Susan. Her brown hand gently touched the sick woman's forehead. Hot and dry. Susan's lips were parched and peeling.

Susan stirred, mumbling under her breath. Her hands came up to push away the covers.

"While we'se waitin' for the doctor, let's make her more comfortable," Em said. "Chance, will you fetch me a fresh basin of cool water? Not cold, now. Cool."

Chance picked up the basin on the bedside table and headed for the door. Wyatt hovered at the end of the bed, tormented eyes on Susan.

Moments after Chance left, the door eased open and Dr. Leatherwood stepped inside. Built like a professional boxer, the medical man removed his black felt hat to expose a shiny bald head. The baldness was a trick of nature, for the doctor had a mere five years' advance on Wyatt.

"Doc!" Wyatt reached out to grasp the doctor's hand like a drowning man reaching for a lifeline. "She's delirious. Is there anything you can do?"

Leatherwood shook Wyatt's hand briefly and shrugged out of his worn black coat. "Let me take a look at her, Hammond." His voice had the calm quality of a man in charge. "Step outside for a few minutes." He spoke to Em. "I'll need your help, ma'am, if you don't mind."

Fifteen minutes later, the doctor opened the bedroom door and called Wyatt inside.

"She's got double pneumonia, Wyatt," he stated.

Wyatt's face sagged. He seemed on the verge of collapse.

The doctor went on, "I've had some success with poultices in cases like this, but there's no way to tell how she'll respond." He spoke to Em. "I'll write down some directions for you to follow. The next twenty-four hours are crucial. I'll be back first thing in the morning to see how she's doing." He pulled a small pad and pencil from his pocket and sank to the rocking chair, talking as he wrote. "Do you have any onions?"

Anxious eyes on his bride, Wyatt stroked his bearded cheek with the back of his hand. "We have about a hundred pounds in the root cellar. We harvested them last week."

"Excellent." He held the page out to Wyatt. "Onion poultices are a lot of work, but I've had better luck with them than mustard plasters."

"Thanks, Doc," Wyatt said as Leatherwood reached for his coat and hat.

"That's what I'm here for," the doctor answered. "I wish I could do more." Putting on his hat, he picked up his black bag and left the room.

Em eyed Wyatt with the expression she used when reminding Jeremy to wash behind his ears. "Mr. Wyatt, this'll take all day and maybe all night. You get yourself to bed before we have to carry you there. Chance can read that paper and tell me what to do."

Wyatt shook his head, refusing though he seemed scarcely to hear. He knelt beside the bed and held Susan's limp hand to his lips. "Don't leave me, Susan. We've hardly begun life together. Don't leave me." He laid his forehead against the quilt.

Em squeezed his brawny shoulder. She resorted to pleading. "Please, Mr. Wyatt. You'll take sick your ownself if you don't rest." She drew the slip of paper from his fingers and pulled at his arm.

Like an aged man, he stood.

Susan turned her head to look at him with dull eyes. "Pa, my bridle's broken again. Can you fix it for me?" Her hand pulled from Wyatt's clasp and plucked at the quilt.

Head bowed, Wyatt plodded from the room in an exhausted daze. He opened the middle door off the living room and trudged inside. Two steps behind him, Em could see a narrow bed and chest of drawers before he closed the door behind him.

"I'd best be gettin' back, Em," Banjo said, rising from the sofa as Em reached him. "Here's your clothes case." He indicated the cloth bag beside the sofa. "Do you need anything else?"

"Only a miracle, Banjo," Em replied, sadly.

"The Chamberlin house will be beggin' God for just that. Let's pray before I leave." Three minutes later, he uttered a quick good-bye, pulled on his hat, and strode outside.

Walking through the hall running from the front door to the back of the house, Em stepped into a spacious square room, a place to feed many mouths. Chance met Em at the kitchen door. "What'd the doc say?"

"He said to follow these directions." She held up the paper. "Bring us some onions."

"How many?"

"All of them."

"All of them? There must be a hundred pounds in the root cellar."

"Read this."

Flattening the paper between his slim fingers, he glanced over it before reading aloud.

"It says, 'Slice onions and place in a frying pan with a little water. Stir and cook until the onions are transparent. Let cool slightly then place them in a clean cotton cloth and apply to the patient's chest and back. Put on fresh poultices every half hour until the phlegm breaks loose. This could take from ten to twenty-four hours.' " He laid the paper on the table, saying, "Looks like it's going to be a long day."

While he fetched the onions, Em lifted a square cast-iron skillet from a hook above the wide six-burner stove. A wall of cabinets covered the east wall. Opening doors, she found two pottery mixing bowls. Chance soon appeared with a fifty-pound sack of onions in his arms. He set it on the floor and turned back to the root cellar. "May as well get the other'n now while I have the strength."

"Wait a minute," Em called. "Where can I find some knives and cotton cloths?"

"Check those drawers." He pointed toward the counter on the left as he hurried away.

After a frantic rush to get started, the process became a monotonous routine. Rolling Susan over to replace the poultice under her back. . .bathing her face. . .stopping her from pulling off the covers. . .praying. . .praying. . .praying.

Wyatt slept until late afternoon. Deep black rings formed around his eyes, and he seemed glued to the rocking chair close to Susan's head, where he could hold her hand and speak into her ear. Em's heart ached for him as much as for Susan, for Em had felt the same pain many years before.

Soon after Katie Littlejohn had married Silas Wescott, Em caught the eye of a young blacksmith named John Bob, a lighthearted, laughing creature with a strong, serious, sensitive soul. Bursting with happiness, Em confided in Katie, who rushed to Silas, coaxing and pleading until her defenseless new husband gave the slaves permission to wed. The law forbade slaves to marry, but regardless of that, Katie had the parlor decorated with flowers and the family held a wedding ceremony. With Master Wescott officiating, the honored couple finished off their vows with the slave tradition of "jumping the broom."

In the truest sense, Em and John Bob had a common-law marriage. Em could not change her name.

Em had always lived with people who loved her, but those months with John Bob were a series of warm, rose-colored moments, a touch of heaven. Master Wescott gave them a private room in the slave quarters—a two-story dormitory behind the house. In spite of their bondage, John Bob and Em had bright hopes for their future in the Wescott household.

Eight months later, a horse kicked John Bob in the head while he bent to nail on a horseshoe. He died the next morning.

Grief brought on preterm labor, and Em's tiny son never drew his first breath. The next day, Em's dreams were sewn into the same canvas and covered with earth.

Wyatt's tears over his delirious bride put a fresh edge to Em's pain that had dulled to bearable levels twenty years before. She'd known deep sorrow several times since, but nothing to match the gut-wrenching agony of that day.

Tears filled her eyes and spilled over. She slipped from the room. The cowhide sofa seemed a good refuge. She sank into its comforting depths and covered her face with her calloused hands.

"What is it, Emma?" His voice heavy with concern, Chance knelt near her, a bowl of water for the sickroom in his hands. "Is she worse?"

Em shook her head. She'd hoped to be alone. How humiliating for Chance to come on her like this! She reached into her sleeve for a handkerchief to mop her eyes.

"No, Chance. Miss Susan's the same. It's me I'se a-crying for. Watching Mr. Wyatt with his poor, sick wife dug up some bad memories." Briefly, haltingly, she told her story.

"You'd best take that water to the bedroom, Chance," she said when she was through. "I'll fetch the next poultice." Stuffing her handkerchief into her sleeve, she trotted to the kitchen. She'd told Chance more than she'd intended. Action gave her an excuse to get away from the painful subject. She hadn't mentioned John Bob's name for fifteen years.

Though the whole house reeked of onions, pungent air slammed into Em's senses when she reached the kitchen. She wrinkled her nose, fighting against burning sensations on sensitive membranes. The first onion sack reclined, half-empty, on the floor, its untouched partner propped nearby. The skillet languidly steamed on the stove. Brown orbs adorned the massive work table in every form from half-peeled to sliced.

With shaky hands, Em picked up a cold poultice lying on the table and took it to the five-gallon bucket filled with cooked onions outside the back door. She was startled to see stars and a brilliant moon. All sense of time vanished in the sickroom.

She folded back the white cotton fabric and shook limp onions on top of their fellows in the pail. Spreading the cloth on the counter by the stove, she spooned hot stringy onions to the center and deftly folded it into a neat flat package.

Chance returned to the kitchen while she prepared the second poultice. He perched on the stool near the mound of raw onions and picked up a small knife. Feeling awkward after her unusual display of emotion, Em concentrated on her work. Inside the cookstove a pine knot popped. The fire made the kitchen warm and close on this mid-September evening.

Chance sliced the onions in even layers. His eyes were clear, unaffected by the tear-jerking vegetable before him. When he spoke it was as though Em's story had never happened.

"I meant to call on you yesterday, Emma, but Miss Susan felt poorly. I couldn't leave her with the kitchen work. It seemed like she got worse by the hour."

"When you didn't come," Em hurriedly replied, "I had a notion something had happened." She dropped two steaming poultices on a plate and hurried to the bedroom. Why did she feel all thumbs and left feet? Mentally, she shook herself. She'd come to the Rocking H to nurse Miss Susan and that's all she'd think about.

Em slipped into the sickroom to find Wyatt just as she'd left him. Susan's face glistened, her face flushed from the heat of the onions.

"It's time to change the onion packs, Mr. Wyatt," Em said softly. "Can you help me turn her over?"

Awaking as a man from a dream, Wyatt put loving arms around Susan and pulled her straight up, her chin resting awkwardly on his shoulder. The movement sent a spasm through her thin frame. With a choking gasp, she coughed violently until tears streamed down her cheeks.

"Lean her over so she can cough it out," Em ordered.

Five minutes later, Wyatt laid Susan back. She melted into the pillow, utterly exhausted. Em gently wiped the moist, sleeping face.

Wyatt relaxed into the rocking chair. His arms hung limply over the sides and toward the floor; his head rested against the chair's high back. "Does the coughing mean anything?" he whispered.

"It's a mighty good sign," Em announced, a weary smile on her lined face. "I don't think she's brought up enough to say she's out of the woods, but we'll keep workin' on her. Jesus will do the rest."

In the kitchen, Chance heaved a relieved sigh when Em told him what had happened. "That's our first good news." He drew a red bandanna from his hip pocket to wipe his face. "I tell you, Emma, this is almost as much work as mining. And mining will kill a man if he doesn't pace himself."

"Minin'?" Em poured a glass of water from an enamel pitcher and perched on a stool across from Chance. An impatient rooster crowed. Em glanced at the clock on the shelf above the sink: 4:00 A.M.

Waiting for Chance to say more, she watched him slice through an onion with rapid, lithe movements. Eyes on his work, he spoke a moment later, "I've got me a claim ten miles northeast of here by Fox Hole Creek. Been working it every Sunday for the past year, some Saturdays, too."

"You find anything?"

"A little," Chance hedged, avoiding her eyes. "I've got a sack of silver nuggets. I'm not sure how much they're worth because I haven't turned anything in yet." He scooped the acrid pile before him into a glazed yellow bowl and picked up another onion. "I don't want the news getting out that there's silver in these parts. Every speculator for fifty miles would be up there in a day's time if I take the nuggets to town."

He paused, noting Em's absorbed expression. "I want to save enough money to buy a few acres and set up a farm. A small place with enough pasture to keep a couple of cows for beef and milk and some planting land besides. I could put in wheat or corn to sell." He grinned, a little sheepish. "You probably have me pegged for a dreamer."

"If so, you'se the good kind," Em said, warming to him. "I wish you well, Chance. I truly do."

A call from the bedroom brought Em to her feet.

"Em! Come quick!"

Em raced down the hall and through the living room, her heart keeping time with her feet. The sound of retching met her at the bedroom door.

"Keep her head down!" she ordered. She grasped Susan's forehead, supporting her. "This isn't pleasant, Mr. Wyatt, but it's just what she needs. I think she's gonna pull through."

six

Two hours later, Wyatt's insistent whisper brought Em's chin up from her chest. She sat in the rocking chair next to the sickbed. "Em! Go to bed. I'll sit with Susan."

Blinking, Em slowly focused on her patient. Susan's breathing came soft and gentle. She lay peacefully in normal sleep. Light penetrated the gauze curtains.

Wyatt hovered over Em's rocking chair. "Your things are in the front room," he said. "You haven't rested in over twenty-four hours."

Em looked up at the young husband. Her bleary mind suddenly realized that Wyatt wanted to be with Susan when she awoke. Em nodded. "That's fine, Mr. Wyatt. I b'lieve I'll do as you say."

Inside the small unadorned bedroom, Em eased back on the goose-down pillow and pulled up the quilt. Her eyes drifted closed. The rope-hung mattress felt heavenly.

≈

Em awoke to the tempting aroma of simmering beef. She stretched and relaxed, allowing herself the little-known luxury of quiet wakefulness. Her mind wandered from Susan's recovery to Chance and his confidences of last night. The man was much more complex than she had first imagined. Interesting. Intriguing.

Her gnawing stomach finally persuaded her to throw back the quilt and bathe her face in the basin on the dry sink. She drew a fresh dress from the carpet bag and smoothed a hand over her neat cornrows.

Wyatt held a finger to his lips when she peeked into the master bedroom. He nodded and smiled in answer to her questioning glance at Susan's sleeping form. Stepping back, Em gently closed the bedroom door.

Chance was scooping stew into serving bowls as she reached the kitchen. Seeing her, his drawn face lightened into a smile. All visible traces of their onion vigil had disappeared. Bubbling beef had banished the acrid smell.

"Good morning!" He glanced at the clock. "Or is it afternoon? Only two minutes' difference right now."

"What can I do to help?"

"Those biscuits need to come out of the pan."

With a broad knife she lifted hot biscuits from a pan on the counter and piled them on two plates waiting nearby. Shaking a finger that got too close to hot metal, she said, "I feel like a piker, going off to bed while you'se still working."

"I'll sleep after the lunch dishes are washed. It's not the first time I've worked the clock around. Won't be the last neither." He set down the stew pot and reached into a drawer for three giant spoons. "I've got some chicken broth simmering on the back of the stove for Miss Susan whenever she wants it." He picked up two steaming dishes. "You could get that door for me, if you don't mind." He bent his head toward the entrance to the north porch, where the hands ate.

Em grabbed the remaining bowl of stew and hurried before him to open the door. The rumble of men's voices met her on the other side.

The porch was a narrow room tacked on the back of the ranch house. Ten feet wide, it ran behind the kitchen, dining room, and part of the master bedroom. Ten feet had been partitioned off the end behind the kitchen to make Chance's quarters.

The now-idle Franklin stove near the kitchen door heated this area built of bare board walls and floor. A plank table ran almost the full length of the room, though at this time of year it was less than half full at mealtimes. The only noticeable feature in the rough room were the windows, five wide ones across the back.

Curly occupied the head seat, flanked by Slim and Amos—who'd beat Jack Savage at arm wrestling. Beside slouching Amos, Brent Cavenaugh cut a fine figure. After six hours in the saddle, his black-checked shirt seemed freshly laundered, the black bandanna knot positioned exactly halfway between Adam's apple and ear. His shapely fingertips brushed the brown birthmark below his right ear as he talked to the husky farm boy next to him. Across from Cavenaugh hunkered Jack Savage, as vulgar in appearance as Brent was refined. Savage reeked of horses and stale sweat. Black wiry hair sprang from his skull at odd angles.

Deep in conversation, Curly and Slim leaned together. Curly's words, "beeves," "grazing," "box canyon," popped over the general noise like corn from a hot pot. Amos and Brent chuckled over a private joke. Savage morosely fingered his empty cup. Catching sight of the aproned black man's approach, Slim straightened. His voice cut through the hum. "Howdy, Chance. How's the missus?" All faces turned to catch the answer. The noise died.

"She's much better," Chance said, setting meaty soup at intervals down the plank table. "She passed the crisis about four this morning." A murmur of relief swept through the men.

The coarse voice of Jack Savage seemed almost indecent following so closely on talk of Susan's illness. "Who's your lady friend, Chance?" Savage thought he was laughing, but to Em's ears he brayed. She hadn't liked him the first time she saw him. She liked him less today.

The big man tapped the table with a chipped enamel cup. "Let's have some coffee, boy." When Chance didn't answer, Savage glared at him and spat out, "You understand me?"

The cook cast a lazy glance in his direction and drawled, "Yes, sir, Mr. Savage. I've been learning English since I was born and studying it ever since."

Snickers came from the hands. Savage glowered.

Avoiding Em's eyes, Chance turned toward the kitchen. Em set down her bowl and followed.

Using a dish towel to pad his hand, Chance grabbed the coffeepot and strode back to the porch.

When he returned, Em didn't comment on Savage's crudeness. Why bother? It was something to be endured and ignored. She remembered Susan's words to Megan about the man. Suddenly, Em's respect for the cook grew. Could she deal with Savage as well as Chance had? Her strong hands itched for a rolling pin or an iron skillet.

Chance set plates on the table in the kitchen and made a mock bow. "Care to join me for lunch, m'lady?"

Grinning at his play acting, Em perched on a stool. She watched Chance pick up his fork and stab a chunk of meat.

Quickly, she asked, "Don't you think we'd best pray before we eat?"

He looked up, startled. "Pray? What for?"

"To thank the Lord for bringing Miss Susan through her sickness and thank Him for the food."

"Emma." His words came out low but with a cold edge. "I've never prayed in my life. I don't intend to start now. If God's so good, why'd He treat us so bad?" Sad, smoldering eyes met Em's. He shook his head and lifted the fork. "You go ahead and pray if it makes you feel better. Don't ask me to."

Rebuffed and aching in her spirit, Em bowed with closed eyes. After a silent, ten-second prayer, she methodically cleared her plate. How could she share the gospel with him if he had that attitude?

In a few moments she carried a hot plate and a glass of water to Wyatt in the bedroom. When she came back, she pushed the exhausted king of the kitchen away from his dishpan. "Let me do that! You go and rest."

After a feeble protest, Chance dropped his apron across a stool and stepped inside his room off the back of the kitchen. Em rolled up her sleeves and plunged elbow deep in hot soapy water.

The clock on the living room mantel sounded two low gongs as Em opened the sickroom door. Wyatt was bending over Susan, lifting her so she could sip some water. He glanced up as Em stepped inside. His empty plate lay on the dresser.

"She's awake, Em." He laid his wife gently back and tenderly smiled down at her.

Susan's tired eyes sought out Em. She stretched out a limp hand. Em quickly clasped the weak fingers between her two sturdy hands.

"Wyatt told me what you've done, Em." Her voice had the quality of an aspen in a faint breeze.

"Don't wear yourself out talking, child," Em warned. "Do you feel up to taking some broth?" At Susan's nod, she placed the pale hand on the bed. "I'll fetch some straightaway."

"I'll feed it to her," Wyatt said, reaching for the mug and spoon when Em returned.

"After she rests again, I'll bathe her and get her into fresh clothes," Em said. "Would you like me to sit with her for a while?"

"No, thanks," came Wyatt's quick reply. "Seeing her get over that fever is better'n steak and apple pie to me. I don't want to leave her." He carefully raised half a spoonful of broth to his wife's parched lips.

That evening, after supper, Susan slept deeply, comforted by a warm bath, a fresh gown, and new linens. Wyatt stretched out in the middle room, napping. Em softly rocked in the chair beside the sick woman's bed. Her eyes wandered from Susan to the big windows that met at the corner across the room. With silent tread, she stepped closer and peered around the curtain.

Twilight crept over the landscape, turning the mountains into giant black mounds against a mauve sky. Ridges and crests had distinct outlines as though cut out with an engraving tool.

If Susan keeps gainin' strength, Em thought, *I'll go home in the morning. Megan will be needin' me.* When Wyatt came to relieve her at eight, Em strolled out to the front porch to rest her weary mind in the cool night air. Sinking to one of four wooden rockers, she watched the darkness. Faint creaks marked her back-and-forth motion. Across the yard, light from the bunkhouse stabbed three yellow beams into the night. In a moment the door opened, letting out an oblong splash, blocked an instant later by the figures of three men passing through. Resting her head against the chair's back, Em lazily observed their course across the yard. They perched on the empty hitching rail thirty feet from the house. Matches flared as two of them lit cigarettes.

"Hensler, nex' time you come over, bring me a pouch o' tobaccy." The Missouri drawl belonged to Amos McClintock.

Em's eyes strained to make out their shadowy forms as smoke reached her nose. These must be the three musketeers, as Wyatt called them.

"If Ah remember, Amos," came the answer from the center man. "Mah memory ain't always the best, ya know."

Brent chuckled. "You don't have any trouble if there's whiskey, women, or money in it for you."

Hensler snickered. "Ah kin handle the important stuff. It's the details Ah mess up on." He drew on the cigarette, making a red glow. "You hopped on the trail of that Feiklin filly quick enough, Cavenaugh."

"Lisa's wild as a yearling. She needs to be halter broke."

"Watch out," Link's sarcastic voice warned. "She may halter break you."

Cavenaugh laughed aloud. "No chance of that, Hensler. It's been tried before."

"How 'bout some poker?" Amos asked. "We kin play for matchsticks."

"Sounds good by me," Brent agreed.

The smokers ground out their cigarette butts, and the troop sauntered across the yard. A flash of light, the bang of the door, and the night resumed its cricket chorus.

Em rocked gently.

Sensing a stealthy motion beside her, she jerked around.

"Evening, Emma." Chance's deep, mellow tones wafted through the evening air. "Sorry if I scared you." She peered toward him. Light from the window shone on his shirt as he walked toward her.

She faltered, "I must have dozed for a minute there." Instinctively, her hand touched the knot behind her head, though she knew he couldn't see her clearly.

"I thought I'd come out and rest my nerves a few minutes

before I turn in," he said. "I didn't know you'd found my favorite night spot."

Em sighed. "It's mighty peaceful out here. I can hardly believe I'm out of Baltimore. Have you ever been to a big city, Chance?"

"I passed through St. Louis on my way west. I can't say I was tempted to settle there."

"In Baltimore we roasted in the summer and froze in the winter. Inside the apartment, I mean. The city was crowded and filthy. I can't hope to tell you how relieved me and Miss Megan are to be away from there. Poor Jeremy, too." She laughed softly. "You should see him a-runnin' with that dog."

"He's a fine boy, Emma. You raised him, didn't you?" It was more of a statement than a question.

"His mama died when he was nine. Up until then her and I shared the motherin' of him." She paused. "I love him like he's my own, Chance. Megan, too. I never had any young'uns but them."

They sat in silence, soaking in the night.

"When are you going home?"

"In the mornin', if Miss Susan's gainin' strength."

"Okay if I call on you Saturday?"

"Why, surely."

"Long as there's no more trouble, I'll be there."

❧

After breakfast, Slim brought the buckboard around to the front door.

"A million thanks to you, Em," Wyatt said.

"That's what neighbors is for, Mr. Wyatt." Em picked up her carpetbag and stepped off the porch. She'd already said good-bye to Chance in the kitchen. "If you need me again, I'll come right away."

An hour later, Megan met Em inside the Chamberlins' front door. "How is Susan?" she asked as she placed her cheek next to Em's.

"Mendin'," Em replied. She set down her case and returned the embrace.

Jeremy rushed up for a hug. "I'm glad you're home, Em," he said. "Megan's been awful tired since you left."

Megan made an effort to smile. Shadows rimmed her eyes. Her silky brown hair lay in wisps about her face. "I was tired before she left, Jeremy, so that's not really news."

"Take this bag to my room," Em said to Jeremy, "and I'll get started on the washing right away."

"Not so fast!" Megan protested, pulling Em's arm toward the settee. "First, you have to tell me what happened at the Rocking H."

Em gave a two-minute description of onion poultices and late nights, ending with, "Miss Susan slept all last night and ate some solid food for breakfast." She made to stand up, but Megan held her back.

"What about Chance?"

"Chance? Why he's fine, Miss Megan. He warn't sick a bit."

Megan looked toward the ceiling in mock disgust. "I know that, Em. I want to know if you talked with him."

Em studied her work-hardened hands for a moment. "We did talk. I got to know him better."

"You're troubled about something, aren't you?"

"He said, 'If God's so good, why'd He treat us so bad?' " Her worry mark deepened as she looked into Megan's brown eyes. "He's a fine man, Miss Megan: honest, hard-working, smart. But if he's mad at God I can't hope to see any tomorrows for him and me."

Megan nodded. "You're right about that, Em."

"It's like he's wrapped in a cocoon of bitterness and hate," Em went on. "He can't cut himself loose. I can't cut him loose neither. Only Jesus has the power to snip those threads." She shook her head in a disheartened gesture. "How can I convince the man of that?"

seven

At nine o'clock Saturday morning Em was hanging freshly boiled white clothes on the line when Lobo began barking and making short sprints toward the trail.

"Look, Em," Jeremy called from the porch steps. He had a thick piece of pine and a short knife in his hands. "A buckboard's coming."

Em walked to the end of the row of newly sewn diapers flapping in the gentle breeze. Before her a field of corn stood browned and dry, days away from harvest. The sun shone brightly; the breeze had lost its torrid feel. Em savored the coolness on her face as she gazed along the edge of the cornstalks. A water-wrinkled hand shading her eyes, she suddenly stiffened.

The wagon driver was Chance.

Why had he come so early in the day? Why in the buckboard?

Quickly, she returned to her laundry basket to finish pinning up the final two shirts before he reached the yard. Two horses paced past her as the wagon clattered into the yard, Lobo yapping at its wheels. Lifting the empty basket, Em turned to greet her visitor.

Jeremy called, "Here, Lobo!" from his seat on the steps.

Chance swept off his flat-crowned black hat. "Mornin', Emma. I'm on my way to town to buy supplies. Mr. Wyatt doesn't want to leave Miss Susan, and the rest of the hands are working the range." He glanced at the crowded clothesline. "I was hoping you could ride into Juniper with me if you're not too busy."

Quickly, Em mentally ticked off the chores she'd mapped out for the day. None were essential.

"Give me a few minutes to set supper on the stove and change my dress. I'd like to come along."

A few minutes past ten, Chance handed her up to the buckboard seat and climbed aboard himself. Em wore her new navy dress with a matching spoon bonnet. She'd finished covering the bonnet form with fabric only last evening.

"Be good, Jeremy," Em called to the solemn urchin leaning on the porch rail, "and I'll bring you a peppermint stick!"

Jeremy's dour expression brightened by half but, eyes half closed, he cast sideways glances at Chance every five seconds.

"Enjoy the day!" Megan said, smiling and lifting her hand as the buckboard moved away. She placed her arm around Jeremy's sagging shoulders and squeezed. Looking down, she asked, "Why so glum? You've got the whole day to do nothing but play. Want to take Lobo down to the creek until lunch?"

"Okay," he murmured. He slid the knife into its sheath and stuffed it and the wood into his spacious overalls pocket. "Come on, Lobo." With a final look at the retreating wagon, he set off jogging across the yard, the wolf-faced dog at his side.

Em looked back in time to see boy and canine leave the porch. The sky directly overhead gleamed clean and bright, but to the west a dark mass hid the mountain peaks.

"I hope that storm doesn't move this way," Chance said. "If it does we'll be in for a wettin'."

"Let's not borry trouble before it comes. It's a lovely day."

She retied her bonnet strings. "What's your chore in town?"

"I've got a list to fill at the general store." He smiled at her. "And I'd like to buy you lunch."

She beamed. "That'd be nice, Chance."

The buckboard rocked through dry puddles, across mounds and rolling hills, around giant orange rocks. Soon frost would wipe out the straggling clumps of blue chicory and black-eyed Susans that had survived the dry heat of late August and early September. Sage and pine tingled their noses.

They talked of canning, crops, and Susan's steady recovery as the wagon wound around a long, straight family of Douglas fir interwoven with scrub oak. Before they were ready, Juniper lay before them, nestled between two low hills, a rifle shot from the endless prairie to the east. Chance guided the wagon to a small space along the populated boardwalk near Harper's Emporium. Saturday was a busy day in Juniper.

The dim interior of Harper's seemed crowded when Chance and Em stepped inside. A bell on the door announced their arrival. Three ladies turned to see who stood at the door. Each glanced quickly away without so much as a nod or smile of greeting. Em had seen similar expressions on white faces thousands of times before: a mixture of fear and distaste.

She glanced at Chance, standing close beside her, hat in hand. He avoided eye contact with anyone and studied the stocked shelves behind the counter.

The door behind them jingled as two men stepped inside. One drew up short then edged around the black couple leaving a wide girth. The second man paused near Chance.

Harper—the thin gray man behind the oak counter—busily filled orders alongside a young clerk with pock-scarred cheeks. When the storekeeper finished with someone, he'd say "Who's next?" and another customer would step to the front.

While they waited, Em looked around the small store. The smell of new leather, fresh-ground coffee, and tobacco filled the air. In the left corner near the door a table held two new saddles, some bridles, and spurs. A dozen leather belts hung on the wall above. Three copper-bound barrels—pickles, crackers, and coffee beans—sat in a triangle shape at the far left of the counter, just below the coffee grinder. Most of the merchandise lay on neat shelves covering the wall behind the counter. Harper and his clerk scurried back and forth plucking items from these stacks and dropping them into burlap sacks.

Last in the line of ladies, Mrs. Pleurd collected her change, picked up her sack, and passed within inches of Em, eyes averted. She must have forgotten their introduction at the barbecue.

"Who's next?" Harper asked, scanning the faces of the men. Grasping an empty potato basket, the clerk stepped through the curtained doorway to the rear in search of a refill.

Chance raised a finger and began to step forward. Ignoring him, Harper turned to the cowhand on the right.

"What can I get for you, Jensen?"

"Half a pound of tobaccy and twenty-five rounds of .44's," the short cowpoke drawled, digging into his jeans for a coin.

Em felt Chance tense, saw his jaw clench. Otherwise his placid expression remained intact.

"Grover?" Harper's attention centered on the man beside Chance, a muscular hombre wearing buckskins and a drowsy expression.

"These folks were ahead of me, Harper," the big man announced. His words were slow and cool, like small stones thrown in a quiet pond.

The storekeeper's eyes wandered in Chance's direction. "What can I get for you?"

Em looked up at the man called Grover. He had kind blue eyes that weren't afraid to meet hers. He allowed himself a small smile and nodded politely.

Chance handed the list over the counter. "Mr. Wyatt said to put these things on the Rocking H bill. He'll settle with you when he comes to town. And," he placed a penny on the counter, "I want a bag of peppermint sticks."

Harper nodded, scanning the paper in his hand. In three minutes, he held out a bulging burlap sack along with a small paper bag.

"How long you stayin', Grover?" Harper asked as Chance grasped the rough cloth.

"I'm passin' through to Texas, Harper. I've been trappin' with the Arapahoe this year, and I'm on my way to sell the pelts."

Chance hefted the heavy load and headed for the door, Em behind him.

Noonday sun clawed at their eyes when they reached the boardwalk. Em waited in the shade of the store's awning while Chance set the groceries in the wagon.

Sheriff Feiklin strode past, heavy boots thumping the boardwalk. He didn't hesitate or speak when he overtook the black couple, but Em saw his eyes. Icy blue, they flicked from her to Chance with a hard, calculating gleam. Em swallowed, suddenly nervous. Why did she suddenly feel guilty for standing on Main Street? Uneasy, Em watched the lawman's back until he ducked into his office farther down the street.

A steady stream of people filed by. If possible, they would have walked straight through her. These people were no different than the white folks in Baltimore: after taking her labor for a few pennies, they'd acted as if she was deaf, blind, and without feelings.

She gazed at the stage station across the street where she'd arrived three months ago. At that instant she decided she wouldn't be coming to Juniper often.

"Ready for lunch?" Chance asked brightly, offering Em his arm.

Shaking off gloomy thoughts, she smiled. "Surely," she replied, slipping her hand under his elbow.

They strolled ten paces down Main Street to a two-story wooden structure with a giant sign. In green and gold lettering it proclaimed, Benson's Hotel and World Famous Restaurant.

"Let's see how famous the food is," Chance said, grinning, as he opened the door. His gleaming hair hung in loose curls that brushed the tips of his ears and the edge of his collar.

A red-haired girl in a white bib apron met them just inside.

"We'd like a table, please," Chance told her.

The girl's cheeks flushed. She cleared her throat. "This way, please." Turning, she led them through the room filled with chatting, chuckling people to the farthest dark corner of the dining room. The noise swelled and faded moment by moment.

Set close together, a dozen tables made up the restaurant. They were cut from the same mold: a thick square of wood with four Windsor chairs each. The plank floor added scuffling, tramping noises to constant chatter and clatter of cutlery.

"We have steak, fried potatoes, beans, and biscuits. Apple pie for dessert," the waitress droned. "Or vegetable soup with light bread if you'd rather."

"We'll have steak, beans, and biscuits?" Chance waited for Em's approval. At her nod, he finished with, "Coffee, too, please."

"You come to Juniper often?" Em asked when the waitress left.

"Twice a year, usually," he said, relaxing in the chair.

"That seems like plenty often to me."

"You noticed the friendly welcome?" Chance's sardonic smile had that bitter tinge.

"Why can't they understand that we'se just people like them? We want a family, a decent place to live, and a future for our children. What's so wrong about that?"

"You've just asked a whopper of a question, Emma. The man who comes up with the answer should have a marble likeness of him set in Washington." Shrugging, he changed the subject. "Tell me, do you ever use saleratus when you're cooking beans?"

They continued trading culinary secrets, discussing the merits of sourdough over yeast an hour later as the buckboard moved south on Main, headed for home. They passed Hohner's blacksmith shop, and the horses picked up their pace.

"I feel guilty leaving Megan again so soon," Em said. The light took on the soft, clear quality of twilight when the sun has sunk behind the mountain yet indirect light still reaches the earth. Today, though, black clouds hid the sun, only an hour past its zenith.

"Did Megan say anything against you coming with me?" Chance asked, suspicion in his voice.

"No. She almost ordered me to go."

"In that case, do you feel too guilty to take a little detour with me before we go back?"

Surprised, Em asked, "Where?"

Chance laughed. It was a soft music that Em loved to hear. "My mining claim. It's three miles west of here." He scanned the sky. "I hope we don't get caught in the rain."

"I don't have to be back till supper, so I reckon I can come along." Em was enjoying herself. If only her nagging doubts about Chance would vanish. She liked his company more than she'd let herself admit. The buckboard lurched off the trail and bounced toward the hills. Em gripped the seat. Her hands ached, then felt numb.

The sky boiled with angry clouds. A chill wind cut through her thin dress, but she was afraid to let go of the seat long enough to pull her shawl about her.

"I'm sorry about the rugged trail, Emma. I usually ride Po'boy over here. It's almost too rough for a buckboard, but we're almost there."

Em drew in a relieved breath when he finally pulled the horses to a stop under a giant cottonwood. "It's over that mound. We'll walk from here."

Grateful to be on solid earth again, Em picked up her shawl and followed him through sagebrush and around wide firs for a hundred yards, watching carefully so she didn't snag her skirt.

"Here it is!" Bending, he pulled away some dry bushes to expose a deep hole in the side of a hill.

"A cave?" Em stepped closer, the worry mark showing. "Ain't it dangerous digging under the ground? The whole thing could fall on you."

"This is a natural cave. The actual mine isn't all that deep. Besides, I'm bracing it with timbers." He stepped inside. "Come and see." Scrabbling around on a ledge, he found matches and a hobo lantern made from a rusty tin can with holes punched in the side. It held a stub of candle.

Feeble light cast long flickering shadows on the inky interior. Em felt a creepy cold shiver that didn't come from the approaching storm. Slowly, like stepping on thin ice, she eased inside, her eyes wide. In the shadows to the left she made out a bundle of clothes and a wheelbarrow with a pick and shovel lying inside.

"Here's the vein." Holding the lantern high, he pointed to the right, shoulder high. Em came close, peering at the dark streak. It was as wide as a pencil and led into the uncut earth ahead.

"That's silver? It's black."

"It has to be purified in a smelter before it'll shine." He ran a long finger along the wide line. "It's silver all right. A rich strike." Letting his hand fall to his side, he turned toward her. "In six months' time I should have enough for a nice piece of land and a small house."

A deep rolling boom reached them from outside. Em hustled twenty steps to the opening and peered out to see rain pelting the landscape. She heard Chance's footsteps behind her. When he spoke, she forgot the storm.

"I brought you here for another reason besides seeing the mine, Emma."

A spasm flitted through her stomach. Turning abruptly, she watched him, fearing his next words.

He set the lantern on the ledge and drew near enough to see the curly fringe around her dark eyes. "These past five years I've planned and schemed how I could get a place of my own and be independent—my own meat, crops, a steady income from a farm. I've had it in my mind that I'd be alone there."

He swallowed. "Then I met you." He inched closer. "During our first walk I realized that being alone isn't what I want after all. I want to share life with someone."

Em stared at him, transfixed.

Deep longing on his face, he said, "It's you, Emma. I want to share it with you."

Em's throat tightened until she feared she'd choke. She

backed away from him, from his lonely eyes, from the spell he cast over her. Her emotions ran hither and yon like a rabbit seeking a way out of a hunter's well-laid trap. Was this where she'd gotten herself by spending time with a man who didn't know Jesus? No wonder God warned against being joined with unbelievers. It had seemed so natural to be with Chance, but she hated the thought of hurting him. But could she put Chance above God? She felt her pulse jumping in her neck.

She croaked, "I can't, Chance. You paint a pretty picture. . . but, I can't."

"Why not?" he demanded, disappointment and hurt clouding his eyes.

She hurried on, "In the first place, I can't leave my children. Megan's about to birth that baby. She needs me. Jeremy needs me." She remembered the boy's prank and his sullen mood whenever Chance came around.

"That's not a good reason, Emma," he retorted. "It'll be another year before I've got a place ready with a house and all. By then Megan's baby will be crawling around getting into mischief."

"I'm too old!" The words gushed out unbidden.

Chance stepped toward her, grasped her shoulders and pulled her toward him. His lips found hers for an instant.

She wrenched away. "No!"

"Am I so disgusting?"

"No! It's not that." She was trembling.

"I know what it is!" he barked, his temper flaring. "You've held on to your masters for security all these years and you're scared to break away. That's it, isn't it?" He made it a statement, not a question.

"No!" she protested, her volume rising. "I stayed because they were my family."

Chance's firm lips twisted in disdain. "White folks?"

Indignation tightened her words. "They were my family, Chance. I didn't have no other'n. Can't you understand that?"

"No, Emma. I can't."

Em's voice grew lower, but her words shook with emotion. "I can't marry you because you aren't a believer. I'm a Christian. I can't join my life to someone who scorns the Lord. It wouldn't work."

"Show me a preacher, and I'll join the church."

"That's not what I mean. Being a Christian is a commitment of the heart, not just joining something like you'd join a political party or a posse. It's asking Jesus to take away your sin and make you His child. When you do it, you have to mean it with all your heart."

Jaw hard, eyes glinting, Chance stared at her. A cool damp wind blew inside and put out the light. "We'd best be getting back," was all he said.

The rain stopped as quickly as it came. It left behind chilly breezes and the flavor of freshly washed air. Flipping the warm shawl about her shoulders, Em followed Chance into the light. He stayed ahead of her on the trail back to the buckboard. The journey home was long and cold and silent.

eight

Two weeks overdue, first frost arrived on the last day of September. Thus, the opening day of October marked the beginning of corn harvest. Banjo rode to several ranches and through the town seeking idle hands to join the work. The following day, a Thursday, the Circle C would host a work day—food, fun, and a fiddle provided when the sun sank below the mountain peaks.

Digging a pit for roasting the young cow Steve had butchered, Steve and Banjo labored until stars twinkled above them. In the center of the yard, Jeremy had carefully teepeed long branches for a wide, high bonfire.

Em slid her first six loaves into the oven half an hour before dawn showed its sleepy face above swaying prairie grass. Wives and daughters would accompany their menfolk to help cook lunch and supper as well as work in the field, but Em wanted to get the baking out of the way before they arrived. A work-hungry man could eat half a loaf without knowing it.

On the kitchen floor stood two bushel baskets: one of corn in the husk ready for roasting and another of fresh apples from the orchard of the Running M, Sanders's outfit.

While the second set of bread baked, Em whipped up a dozen eggs. Bacon sizzled and popped in the frying pan. Jeremy crept up behind her and wrapped his arms about her slim waist.

"Good mornin' child," she said, dropping her fork to put an

arm around the boy's shoulders. His hair looked like a new rag mop. "I'll have you a plate ready by the time you wash up. Don't forget. . ."

". . .to wash behind my ears," Jeremy finished, giving her an impish grin. He banged out the back door and returned in two minutes, dragging a black comb through blond tangles.

"Who's comin' today, Em?"

"I don't rightly know, Jeremy." She lifted the last crispy strips from the pan and poured some grease from the skillet into a clean tin can. Clanging the frying pan back to the stove, she poured in a small circle of eggs. "Mr. Wyatt said he'll encourage his hands to come, though the Lord knows cowboys do hate farm work. Miss Susan may come, too, if she's feeling up to it. She won't be doin' any work, though. She and Miss Megan will sit on the sofa and visit."

"Can I have an apple?" he asked, looking over the juicy specimens before him.

"Sure thing, child. Pick out one for yourself."

He lifted two for inspection before deciding on a third. "Here, Em." He held the red fruit toward her. "I want it bald headed."

Em smiled. "Lay it on the counter and I'll peel it while you eat."

He scooted into a chair at the table, cocked his head at her, and asked, "How about Chance? Is he comin'?"

Em tried to act normal, but she felt her face growing tight. "I don't know about Chance, Jeremy. I haven't seen him for two weeks, since I went to Juniper that time."

Leather hinges on the front door groaned as Banjo came through. Glad for a diversion from Jeremy's quizzing, Em added more eggs to the hot pan and picked up a clean plate.

She was pulling the last loaves from the oven when the

Feiklin family arrived. Draped over the kitchen counter were several snowy dish towels. On them lay twenty golden loaves in close rows. Beside the bread stood six dried-apple pies she'd prepared yesterday.

With cheeks and eyes glowing in anticipation of feminine company, Megan opened the door for Sally, who bustled in carrying a cloth-covered basket, Lisa and Jessica close behind her. Through the window, Em noticed Rod Feiklin heading for the cornfield, scythe in hand. Steve, Banjo, and Jeremy were already pulling fat ears from crackling brown stalks. They'd chop the bare corn plants and store them in bins for cattle feed against the coming winter.

"Good morning, Miz Chamberlin." Sally's brassy voice filled the house. "Are we the first ones here?" She set the basket on the table and swiveled her head toward Megan to catch the answer.

Megan glanced out the window. "I believe the Sanders family has just arrived."

Sally leaned toward Jessica, "What did she say?"

Her younger daughter leaned toward her, forming the words carefully, "She said the Sanders family is here."

Sally beamed. "Wonderful. I haven't spoken to Ruth since the barbecue." She picked up the saltshaker and threw a shower of salt over her left shoulder. "We'll need some luck today." Setting the tin container down, she snapped the cloth from the basket. Inside lay two paper sacks and a large bowl stacked with sweet rolls.

Em brought the coffeepot and a nest of cups as Sally placed the sweet rolls in the center of the table, a light breakfast for the ladies. Later, one of the girls would carry cold water and buns to the field for the men.

Within the hour the modest home seemed crowded. Elaine

Sanders and her mother, Ruth, sat with the Feiklins at the table while they all peeled potatoes.

"Did I ever tell you about the time a young fellow sent me a poem every Sunday?" Sally chirped. "He'd tie the paper to a stone and throw it through my bedroom window."

"Do you remember any of the words to them?" Elaine asked.

Lisa laughed. "She's got them all in a cigar box tied up with red ribbon."

Sally singsonged, "Sally, I love you. You are my turtledove, you. Your face is a dandy. Your lips as sweet as a gum drop."

Listening from the sofa, Megan winced.

When the titters around the table died down, Ruth spoke. "What happened when the weather turned cold and you had to close your window?"

"Oh, before the summer was over, he pitched one rock too hard and cracked the mirror on my bureau. Daddy made him quit throwing stones. After that he'd slip his poems into a crack on our porch swing and stand outside my window making noises like a hoot owl. That way I knew to go downstairs and look for it." The pudgy woman smiled, remembering. "He did that till he got his feet frozen one night in a heavy snow."

"Didn't you feel sorry for him?" Elaine asked.

"I guess I did," Sally replied. "I've been married to him for twenty-one years."

Astonished looks were followed by another round of merry laughter. Chuckling over the story, Em stepped outside to check the roasting beef in the yard.

She was turning the spit when the Rocking H crew arrived. Wyatt and Susan sat in the front of the buckboard with Brent, Amos, Curly, and Chance in the wagon. Em watched Chance lift a stack of bushel baskets from the buckboard and trudge toward the field. He glanced her way but made no sign that he saw her.

Would he speak to her today? Besides a gruff good-bye when he left her two weeks ago, he hadn't said a word to her since they'd left the cave.

Why did she feel so low when she'd done the right thing?

"I'll turn the handle awhile," Lisa offered at her elbow.

"Thank you, Miss Lisa. My arm could use a rest." For the first time, Em noticed that Lisa had left her hair down.

Not very practical, the older woman mused. Releasing the makeshift spit handle, Em trudged toward the house.

Across the yard, Brent arrived at the Rocking H buckboard for his second load of tools. He lifted a scythe and paused, calculating eyes on Lisa.

Em's lips pursed thoughtfully as she watched Brent saunter in Lisa's direction. Lifting the door latch, Em stepped inside.

Beside the fireplace sat Susan, a mite thin but with roses faintly blooming in her cheeks. Across from her, Megan wove a three-inch strip of lace to put on the edge of a crib coverlet. Susan's smile widened when she saw Em.

"Miss Susan!" Em hurried over to clasp the young woman's hand. "It's good to see you lookin' so well."

"I'm almost back to normal, Em," Susan said. "I still have to nap in the afternoon, but otherwise I'm fine. There's no way I can thank you for all you did."

"That smile is thanks enough!" Em exclaimed. "You all have a nice visit while I look after the food." She bustled into the kitchen.

Potatoes peeled, the teenage girls joined the men pulling corn in the field. Sally tended the beef while Em stirred together a rice pudding and Ruth laid corn in the coals under the roasting cow.

Backs ached and feet felt like lead by the time darkness ended the workday. By twos and threes dusty, weary people trudged into the bonfire's light. Lisa, Elaine, and Jessica arrived together with smudged cheeks and bits of brown husk in their hair. Fatigue hadn't dulled the fire in Lisa's eyes. The girls joined the line in front of the full barrel beside the stable to share a common ladle. The water was cold, freshly drawn from the mountain spring behind the house.

The work lay half finished. Tomorrow Steve, Banjo, and Jeremy would finish the rest with three hired men from town.

Ernie perched on an upended log, tuning his fiddle. Tonight his bow would earn him three dollars.

Chairs from the house stood in the yard for the ladies. Steve and Banjo brought the settee to the porch so Megan and Susan could enjoy the music. Several people found logs to sit on. The rest lounged on the grass or the porch steps.

Ruth and Sally filled the sawhorse table with sliced bread, mountains of potatoes, and long pans of rice pudding dotted with raisins. Em stood beside the sizzling brown beef cutting out hefty chunks and placing them in a bowl at her feet.

"Need some help?" a mellow voice asked.

Em faltered, "You've been working all day, Chance. Sit down and rest yourself."

"I'd rather help you." Gently, he plucked the long fork and knife from her hands. He worked without talking, but it was a different kind of silence from what they'd shared on their ride home from Juniper.

Lifting another long fork from a platter, Em dug corn from the ashes in the pit. The blackened husks crackled as she rolled them out and scooped them into a bowl. Jeremy appeared from the darkness, Lobo at his heels. He jogged past the black couple without stopping to say hello.

After prayer, folks lined up to pass by the food.

"Well, looky here." Banjo's voice rose above the rest. "Step aside, folks, and let me at the spotted pup," he said, eyeing the rice pudding. "I love that stuff almost as much as I love Kelsey, my long-eared donkey."

"There's apple pie for dessert," called someone who'd reached the end of the table. "I'm glad I'm ahead of you all." Chuckles and smiles flitted through the ranks.

Dinner was a festive affair, though it had a different flair from the barbecue. Tired and bedraggled though they were, the laborers found enough energy to play awhile before they scattered across the hills to their homes. Jeremy and Lobo sprawled side by side on the grass beside the porch steps. Ears high, the dog watched for frequent offerings thrown him by his young master.

Em sat on the steps, an empty plate on her lap. Behind her, Megan said, "Susan, are you sure you're not too tired?"

"Don't fuss over me," the young woman replied, laughing lightly. "That nap will hold me till we get home."

The Sanders family left as soon as they finished the meal. They had the longest distance to travel. Em tensed as Chance strode purposefully in her direction, glad he'd come yet wishing he'd go away.

He said, "Would you like to walk awhile?"

Her feet groaned, but Em ignored them. She couldn't bear the tenseness between them, and they needed to talk. Handing her plate to Megan, she stood. "That'd be fine, Chance."

Slowly, aimlessly, they strolled away from the garish light of the fire and a rollicking rendition of "Old Dan Tucker." The sweet odor of cut cornstalks came in waves on the breeze. When her eyes adjusted to the gloom, Em saw two forms ahead of them in the darkness and made out a riotous mass of curling hair—Lisa Feiklin with a man.

"How have you been, Emma?"

"Same as always, I guess," Em answered. "Since the canning got done, things have been quiet around here till today. I'll be pullin' corn tomorrow, I reckon." She searched her mind for a safe topic. "Miss Susan's looking right fine."

"Another week and she'll be riding again, I expect." Chance dismissed the subject and groped for another.

The moon shone like a brilliant silver dollar, shedding smooth, gentle light on the party. It was a hayride moon, a hunting moon, a lover's moon.

When he spoke, his words seemed impatient, as if he wanted to get them over with. "Look, Emma. Do you think we could go back to the way things were before? Before the cave, I mean? These two weeks I've whipped myself day and night for being a brass-plated fool. Can you forgive me?"

Maybe they could salvage a friendship out of this, even if marriage was out of the question. "Surely, Chance. I'd like to forget it ever happened."

He drew a deep breath. "So would I."

Jeremy and Lobo passed them, brushing Chance's elbow.

"Jeremy! Watch where you'se a-goin'," Emma called.

"It's a miracle he can still run," Chance remarked, "after the back-breaking day we've had."

Emma chuckled. "It's a miracle all right." She told him about Jeremy's battle with rheumatic fever.

They walked past the corral and the chicken house before circling back. A chilly breeze skipped through, but quickly left to find other sport. Em wished she'd brought her wrap.

"Would you mind if I still call on you sometimes? As a friend? That is, if you don't mind being friends with an old heathen like me."

"I'd like it fine, Chance. That's what I wanted all along." She drew in a breath of clear air. Oddly, she didn't feel nearly as tired as she had twenty minutes ago.

Out of the darkness, racing Jeremy knocked Chance full in the back, almost knocking him down. The boy fell back, bounced up, and kept running.

"Jeremy Wescott!" Em cried. "What's got into you?" Mortified, she said, "I'm real sorry, Chance."

He worked his shoulders as though stretching. "Nothing's broken, I guess." His expression changed from concern to alarm. Clutching at his back, he twisted around, his movements becoming more frantic by the second.

"What is it?" Em demanded.

"Something's crawling down my shirt!" He slapped behind his shoulder blade.

"Is it stinging you?"

"Not yet." He tugged frantically at his buttons, noted Em's anxious eyes and turned his back toward her. "I apologize, Emma. I can't abide crawly critters. Never could." Slipping out of his shirt, he shook it—then held it up, catching the firelight to check for residents.

The ludicrous situation made Em smile. Chance glanced over his shoulder.

"For shame, Emma! You laughed at me when I had that tomfool flour in my hair and now you're about to do it again."

"I'm afraid Jeremy's up to something," she said, biting her upturned lips. "I'll speak to him about it."

"As Mr. Wyatt says, I'd be much obliged." A hint of sarcasm came through.

An instant later, Em's snickers died.

The glow of the flames reached Chance's bronze back. Instead of the firm, smooth flesh she expected, the thick skin was creased, puckered. Pale lines crisscrossed from shoulder to shoulder, from neck to waist. Scars. Deep, hideous scars.

Tears welled up before Em could stop them. She put out her hand and touched a white streak.

Chance froze. Slowly, he turned and looked at her. Em's swimming eyes gazed mutely into his. He looked away and shrugged into his shirt.

Fastening the buttons, he spoke deliberately. "I took *Clark's Grammar* from Master Pettigrew's library. The foreman found it in my bedding. I didn't steal it. I used to take it every Saturday night to study while the others slept."

Tears spilled over one by one and slid, shining, down Em's brown cheeks.

Naked pain lay grimly detailed on the man's taut face. His lips twitched.

For the first time in twenty years, Em listened to her heart instead of her head. She stepped into his arms.

One wounded creature reaching out to another, they held each other and shared the anguish, the agony that only those who know like affliction can fully understand.

"Forgive me," Em whispered into his shoulder.

"For what?"

"For acting like your past was no account." She drew away and lifted her wet face to him. "I don't know all the answers, Chance. Fact is, I don't know half as many as I thought I did ten minutes ago." She pulled in a shaky breath. "But I do know that Jesus can help you. If only I could explain it to you better."

He placed a finger on her lips, his voice thick with unexpressed emotion. "Let it lie, Emma. Please."

Closing her eyes, she nodded. He lifted her hand and placed it inside his crooked elbow. They took one more slow turn around the yard, not talking but sensing deeper companionship than mere conversation could provide.

Near the fire, Ernie was sawing out "Buffalo Gals" when Wyatt's voice sliced through the music. "The Rocking H wagon is pulling out. Everybody get aboard."

"Okay if I come by next week?" Chance asked.

The woman by his side smiled softly. "I'll bake a cake."

"Gingerbread with icing sugar?"

They laughed. It had an infectious, warm sound. He touched her chin lightly before he turned away.

Em watched him stride toward the stable, where Wyatt and Susan waited in the buckboard. Brent and Lisa lingered beside the wagon, waiting for the last passenger to climb aboard before they said good night.

After the buckboard vanished, Em scanned the yard—now occupied by the Feiklins, Banjo, and Steve—seeking a small boy. Ernie scratched away at the last verse of "Good-bye Ole Paint, I'm A-Leavin' Cheyenne," the usual signal that the party was breathing its last.

On the steps Em collared protesting Jeremy and hauled him into the house, shushing him as they moved so he wouldn't bother Megan, who had already retired. A lighted lantern rested on the mantel shelf.

"Now then, Mr. Jeremy," she whispered fiercely when they reached the empty living room. "What's this about tormenting poor Chance? First flour in his hat and now a bug down his back." Her eyes skewered him. Jeremy stood before her, carefully inspecting his bare toes.

"What's got into you, child?"

Finally, he blurted out, "He's gonna take you away, ain't he, Em?"

"Take me away?" The weary woman repeated. She grasped

the boy's shoulders. He looked up at her, the corners of his mouth pulled down. Leaning toward him until her nose came inches from his, Em said softly, "He's not gonna take me away, Jeremy. You're my boy. Nothin' could ever change that, you hear?"

Jeremy threw his arms around her middle, squeezing the breath out of her. "I couldn't stand it if you went away, Em."

Em pressed him tightly to her heart. *Lord,* she prayed, *this knot's got to be untangled. And You'se the only One Who can do it.*

❧

Sunday morning the Chamberlin family lingered around the breakfast table, relaxing their aching joints and heavy heads. The last of the corn had been bagged and—with the last chopped stalks—had been loaded into the barn at midnight. That was eight hours ago. Every man and woman was anxious for a quiet, restful day.

"Six hundred bushels from twenty-five acres ain't bad, Chamberlin," Banjo remarked.

"A bumper year," Steve agreed, stretching back in the chair, legs straight out before him. "Let it rain buckets now. The better to sleep by."

Beside him Megan chided, "Now, Steve. You've never slept in the daytime in your life."

"I feel like today'd be a good startin' place." He sipped his third cup of coffee.

"A rider," Banjo announced, leaning back to look out the window. "Looks like one of Hammond's men."

"I hope Susan's not sick again," Megan worried. "I'm afraid she overdid herself by coming Thursday."

Jeremy scampered out the door without closing it behind him, hoping to take care of the man's horse. The rider turned out to be Wyatt himself. He tossed the reins to Jeremy and strode to the house. Hat in hand, the rancher stepped inside.

"Mornin', Wyatt," Steve called from his seat. "Come on in and take a chair. We're actin' like rich folks over breakfast. Been sittin' here for an hour or more. Care for some coffee?"

"That would hit the spot." Wyatt took a place next to Banjo and reached for the full cup Em offered. He took a long sip and sighed. "The field looks good. You finish last night?"

"At midnight," Steve said. He handed Wyatt a plate with two biscuits left on it.

"How's Susan?" Megan asked.

Their guest split a biscuit and smeared it with freshly churned butter. "I left her scrubbing breakfast dishes. We had us a full-fledged squall this morning. Chance didn't come back after his days off, and she insisted on cooking for the hands." He chuckled softly. "When a woman gets her dander up, Chamberlin, there's no talkin' her down."

"Where's Chance?" Megan asked, impatient for news.

"Nobody knows. To make matters worse, we got a visit from Sheriff Feiklin at first light this mornin'. Late Friday night some hombre robbed the stage to Cedar Grove. He got away with ten thousand dollars in coin and silver nuggets. Witnesses say the robber was a black man."

nine

Em laid aside her dishcloth and stood beside the table near Megan's chair while Wyatt continued his story.

"Feiklin searched Chance's room and found a sack filled with silver nuggets. Three thousand dollars worth, according to him."

Em interrupted. She couldn't bear to hear more. "Chance got those nuggets from a mine in the hills. He took me there on our way back from Juniper. Chance would never steal!"

"Susan and I agree with you, Em. That's why I rode over. I knew you and Chance have been friendly, and I was hoping you could give me a clue where Chance might have gone."

"Why didn't he come home last night?" she asked.

"The sheriff told us that Chance showed up in Juniper on Saturday afternoon. He went into Harper's store and bought a shovel. Somebody saw him ride in. They rounded up a posse to shanghai Chance when he came back into the street.

"When Chance realized what the gang was up to, he knocked down two of them with the shovel, cut open a third man's head, and lit out on Po'boy. Two of the jaspers found a couple of empty saddles and took out after him. They lost him in the hills. No one's seen hide nor hair of him since." Hammond drummed his fingertips on the table. "Unfortunately, the sheriff takes that as a sign he's guilty."

Em's worry mark widened. She pulled out a chair and

plopped into it as though her knees had given out. Four pairs of eyes watched her. Four pairs of ears waited for her to speak.

She stared out the window. A brown sparrow walked across the outer sill, head bobbing forward at each step. When it reached the edge, it leapt into the air, body curved, tail spread, and wings wide. Em sighed twice. Finally, she faced Wyatt. "If I tell you where he is, what will you do?"

"Just talk to him, Em. If he gives me his word that he didn't rob the stage, I'll believe him. But, remember, whether he's guilty or not, the safest plan is for him to surrender to Sheriff Feiklin and stand trial. Then his name will be cleared."

"What if he don't agree to that?"

"I won't force him to do anything, Em. I can't force him."

"You could turn him in."

Wyatt's eyes crinkled as his words intensified. "That's the last thing I want to do. Please believe me."

Em searched his open, concerned face for a long moment.

Banjo leaned forward, his forearm on the table. "Chance needs some friends right now, Em. Who else will help him if we don't?"

"Will you go along, Banjo?" Em asked.

"Be glad to."

She turned back to Wyatt. The lines on her face had deepened. Her eyes were pools of pain. "I want to go, too."

"That's okay by me," Wyatt said, stroking his beard.

Megan and Steve were solemn spectators to the drama unfolding before them. Megan reached out to clasp Em's hand as the troubled woman spoke.

"He's probably in the cave near Fox Hole Creek where his mine is. I saw some food and clothing stored there. The cave's hidden, so he'd likely think it's the safest place."

Banjo asked, "Can you find it again?"

"I reckon so. At least comin' from Juniper way I could."

Megan squeezed Em's hand and said, "I'll take care of the house today."

Steve intervened, his expression a mixture of love and resolve. "You mean Jeremy and I will take care of the house, little lady. You didn't sleep till way past midnight last night."

Megan ruefully smiled at her second mother. "I couldn't get comfortable. I feel like a lumpy sack of potatoes these days."

"I hate to leave you, honey," Em said.

Banjo stood and scraped his chair back. "If the cave's between here and Juniper, we shouldn't be gone long, Em."

Megan reached out to Em for a hug. "Go ahead with the men. Steve will take your place bossing me today. You can have your turn when you get back."

Em gave Megan a squeeze and got to her feet. She headed into the kitchen to pack some food. Chance would surely be hungry by now.

In the buckboard, Banjo and Em crossed the creek with Jeremy and Lobo trailing behind it. Wyatt rode his sleek palomino, Ben. Boy and dog stopped for a rough-and-tumble before racing back toward the house. The cornfield lay full of awkward stubbles.

Few words passed between them on the journey. Em twisted her hands together and focused on the horizon, oblivious to the sharp-edged smell of autumn, the brown foliage razed by frost. Only the firs and pines remained clothed in deep green—like soldiers in proud uniform.

"It was somewhere in here," Em decided a little more than an hour later. She peered west, straining to find a familiar boulder or tree. "There it is! See the spot where the trail widens?"

The buckboard rattled and jolted around the turn.

Beside her, Banjo remarked, "With this racket, he'll light out before we get there."

"We'll have to walk a good ways," Em said. "I doubt he can hear the wagon from where we have to stop."

The closer they drew to the cave, the more anxious she became. Would Chance trust Wyatt and Banjo enough to let them help him?

"We walk from here," she announced ten minutes later. The cottonwood's spreading limbs held limp, drab scraps of what had been brilliant gold only two weeks ago. A few more days and all its leaves would lie scattered about the hillside.

Em gnawed her lip. Her face was seamed with worry as she stepped to the ground. "How about if I go up first and talk with him alone?" she asked.

"You're calling the shots, Em," Wyatt said. His proud stallion stood ground hitched nearby. "If that's what you want, we'll wait here. Give a holler when you're ready for us." The men followed her for a dozen paces then turned to the left to rest on a fallen log.

Heart thumping dully, Em slowly wound around the sage-strewn incline. Thirty feet from the cave entrance she stopped and called, "Chance! It's Em! I need to talk to you."

Heavy silence answered her. Listening to her own breathing, she waited.

Ten heartbeats later, his uncertain voice called, "You alone, Emma?"

"Look outside and see for yourself," she called. "I came because I want to help you, Chance."

"Come on in." He spoke like a condemned man waiting to hear his sentence.

Em reached the door of the cave and pulled a small

crackling bush from the edge of the mound before her. Chance's strong hands reached out to widen the gap for her.

She stepped inside, peering at his gaunt, weary face through the dim light. "You okay? You gave me the scare of my life."

"I gave you a scare? I haven't been sittin' up here enjoying the scenery."

To the left lay a rumpled coat that looked as if it had been used as a blanket. The hobo's lantern lay cold and dark on its shelf. A tall bay gelding stood hobbled and snubbed up short by the far right wall.

"I came to hear your story," she told him. "Mr. Wyatt rode in this morning to tell us what happened. He thinks you're innocent, Chance. He says he wants to help you."

"You sure he isn't just trying to find out where I am so he can tell Feiklin?"

Em studied his haggard face before saying, "Mr. Wyatt's your boss man. You'll know the answer to that if you study on it awhile."

The gelding stamped and sidled away from the wall. His saddle lay on the ground a short distance away.

Bottom lip thrust forward, Chance said, "If somebody would let me prove where I was when the robbery happened, I might be able to clear myself." He shrugged. "Maybe. I don't even know when the holdup happened."

"I know someone who wants to hear what you have to say."

"Who?"

"Banjo and Mr. Wyatt." Em's chin came up. "They're waiting outside." She raised her hand. "Simmer down, Chance. They want to help you."

Chance grimaced. "Sure." He sounded anything but sure.

Em's temper blossomed. "Use them smart brains in your

head, man! While you're thinking, think about this: if they don't help you, who will? You can't hide here all winter. You'll freeze. And what'll you eat?" She held out the sack of food in her hands. "I brought you this, but it won't last over two days."

Immediately, he lost interest in the argument. Taking the sack, he peered inside, holding the wide mouth sideways to catch the light. "You're a saint, Emma," he murmured. He lifted out a slab of beef and bread wrapped in a light cloth and, setting the canvas aside, lost half his face in the sandwich.

Em's heart twisted. The man must be half starved. While he ate, she took stock of her surroundings. A dented pail, pick, and shovel lay inside a wheelbarrow. Two empty tins and a canteen lay beside the rumpled coat, but she could detect no traces of a cooking fire.

Swallowing the last crumb, he said, "I've had two cans of peaches, some cold beans, and two hard biscuits these past two days. At night I sneak down to the creek to fill my canteen."

She pushed away the sentimental feelings gripping her. She must talk reason to him. Her question had a hard edge. "You think things'll get easier from here?"

His shoulders sagged. "Bring the men in."

Em gripped his arm, her expression softening. "You won't be sorry, Chance. Banjo and Mr. Wyatt are right as rain."

"I feel like a rat in a barrel. I don't even have a gun."

Three minutes later, Em entered the makeshift doorway with two men ducking in behind her. Chance stood five paces back in the darkness of the cave, his jaw hard, his eyes narrowed.

Banjo paused a moment, squinting eyes trying to adjust to the dimness. He stepped forward, hand outstretched. "Howdy, Chance. You're a sight for sore eyes. For a while there, I was afraid you wouldn't talk to us."

Chance shook Banjo's hand and quickly dropped it.

The old veteran went on, "We want to help you. Both Wyatt and I can read signs and we thought we may be able to pick up some clues the sheriff won't find."

Of course, they could read tracks. *Why didn't I think of that before?* Em wondered. Hope rose in her heart.

Banjo went on, "Feiklin's honest as the day, but he's always in a hurry. If he's satisfied that he knows who's guilty, he won't look any further."

Wyatt added, "We want to hear what you have to say, Chance. Susan's worried half to death about you."

At the mention of Susan's name, the black man relaxed a little. "How's Miss Susan getting along? I'm sorry to have to leave her with the cooking."

"She's in fine fettle," Wyatt said, grinning. "We had a big ruckus this morning. She insisted on cooking for the men. I tried to talk her out of it, but short of dragging her out by the hair, I couldn't make any headway." He chuckled. "She finally picked up a cast-iron spider pan and chased me out of the house. Said not to come back till I found you and did something to help."

Chance drew in a long breath. He wanted to go home. "Let's sit down," the wanted man said, moving two steps toward the front, where more light trickled in.

Perched on the hard-packed earth, Chance rubbed his face with both hands in an agitated gesture. Wyatt and Banjo sat across from him, but Em remained standing. She refused to soil her dress by sitting on the ground. The horse swished his tail and blew.

"When did the robbery happen?" Chance rasped out.

Wyatt answered, "Friday evening after sundown. The

holdup man stopped the stage where the road to Cedar Grove cuts through the woods. The road runs along our south property line at that spot."

The hunted man gazed into the middle distance, considering. "I'd turned in by that time, I reckon. Miss Susan gave me the whole of Saturday off. I wanted to head out before first light, so I went to bed right after the supper dishes."

Banjo grunted. "That cuts out an alibi. Where did you go when you left home?"

"Up here. I worked till past noon, when my shovel hit a stone and a big piece of metal chipped off. I rode into town to buy another one. When I came out of Harper's store, a bunch of men tried to jump me. They said I'd robbed a stage and called me some names I'd rather not repeat. One of them shouted that they ought to string me up." He paused, sweat beading on his forehead.

Em's throat tightened. She hid her trembling hands in the pockets of her skirt.

Chance went on, "I guess I panicked. I swung at them with the shovel, knocked a couple down, and ran for Po'boy. That horse has bottom, I tell you. He lit out of there like a jackrabbit with his tail on fire and didn't quit till we got to Fox Hole Creek.

"I circled wide around and came back here. I've been here ever since."

"Who jumped you?" Wyatt asked. "Did you know the men?"

"Link Hensler was the ringleader. He was the one promoting a necktie party. I've seen the other four a few times, but I don't know their names."

Banjo spoke up. "Where'd you get them silver nuggets?"

"You're looking at the place. I've been working this mine for more than a year. I haven't turned in any ore because I was afraid there'd be a run on the area if the news got out that I'd made a strike."

"Sheriff Feiklin found your nuggets, Chance," Wyatt said. "He took the sack with him as evidence."

Chance's head jerked around. His nostrils flared out. "Evidence! Evidence of what? That silver cost me sweat and blood." Chest heaving, he glared at the bearded man across from him. "What right did he have to take my silver?"

"The stage carried ten thousand in coin and silver nuggets," Wyatt continued calmly, "so finding a sack of nuggets in your room looks mighty bad." He scratched the back of his neck. "I wish you hadn't kept your mine a secret, Chance. But it's all water over the dam now. We'll have to go on from here."

Em's voice made them crane their necks upward. "Can you all do anything to help him?"

"We can try to track down the guilty cuss," Banjo replied, grimly. "The thief was no stranger to Juniper. How many folks know that the Rocking H has a black cook, that the road to Cedar Grove passes by the backside of the ranch, and that the stage was carrying so much money?"

Banjo got to his feet and dusted the backside of his pants. "We'd best be movin' on. I'd like to ride into Juniper and talk to the stage manager, Buckeye Mullins. He's a friend of mine."

Em stepped closer to Chance as he stood up. "Is there anything you need?" she asked.

"A couple blankets and some hot food. I'm afraid to build a fire in case someone comes nosing around." He turned to Wyatt. "Can you take my horse home? I can't keep him. There's no food for him here."

Banjo spoke up. "How about if I turn him into the box canyon with our beeves? Feiklin will be less likely to find him there."

"I'm obliged," Chance said, shortly. His attitude had improved slightly, but he wasn't bursting with warm friendship. He strode to Po'boy, speaking softly as he untied the knots.

"Chance," Wyatt said, grasping Po'boy's bridle, "we'll do what we can."

Banjo lifted the saddle. Men and horse slipped through the doorway, but Em waited. She wanted to say something comforting before she left. But what?

Finally she blurted out, "Take care of yourself. I'll see you in a couple days."

He stared. His face turned hard and cold. "If they put out a reward on me, I'll swing from a rope. Maybe it's just as well. From where I stand, living isn't such a treat. I'm tired of being kicked around. Go on home, Emma. I'll be just fine. And you can tell your friends I'm not worth helping. Not that they intend to help me anyway."

ten

After Banjo and Wyatt carried Em back to the Circle C, Banjo saddled Kelsey. The men paused long enough to swallow a sandwich and a bowl of Megan's turnip soup before dusting off to Juniper.

Em scarcely touched her lunch. She stared glumly at the blue gingham hanging beside the dining room window.

Gathering, scraping, and stacking dirty plates, Megan asked, "Are you okay, Em? You haven't said three words since you came home."

Em laid her spoon on top of Megan's pile. "I keep seeing Chance standing in that dark cave. He looked like he'd lost his last friend. I reckon he thinks he has, Miss Megan. He don't rightly trust Banjo and Mr. Wyatt." She sighed. "Even if those fellers find the real thief, Chance is so bitter and twisted up inside that I doubt he'll ever turn to the Lord."

Megan pulled out the chair next to Em and sat. Eleven days from the projected end of her vigil, her movements were awkward, her face puffy with added pounds. She reached for Em's strong hand lying limply on the oak table. "Things look bad, Em. But I know God can turn it around for good. Let's pray about it right now." She closed her eyes.

Em dipped hot water from the reservoir at the back of the stove and poured it into a basin. Megan trundled to the bedroom for her prescribed afternoon nap.

A few moments later, a shout drew the weary black woman to the window.

"Anybody home?" It was a resonating voice, as if it came from the inside of a cracker barrel.

Em felt close to panic when she peeked through the window and recognized Sheriff Rod Feiklin. He stood at the porch steps. His horse, a blue roan with an apron face, cropped grass ten feet behind him. The lawman held his tan Montana slope, and wisps of gray hair lay plastered across his pink skull. Like his jeans and blue flannel shirt, his hat showed plenty of mileage.

"Chamberlin!"

Like a young'un expecting a lickin', Em moved to the door and gently lifted the latch. "Miss Megan's restin'," she said, stepping outside. "Mr. Steve is on the range today."

Five feet eight and two hundred pounds, the man before her stood wide in the body, thick in the neck, and deep in the chest. His round florid face hung down in big jowls with a permanent five o'clock shadow. He wore a scuffed cowhide vest sporting a shiny silver star.

Feiklin didn't smile or greet her. He merely grunted, "I reckon it's you I want to talk to anyway."

Em trod to the top of the stairs. She rubbed the inside of her fingers with a nervous thumbnail.

"I saw you walkin' out with Hammond's cook at the corn harvest. One gets you fifty, you know where he ran off to." He stood with his shoulders thrown back, his feet planted, and his jaw tilted upward. His large, lumpy nose had red veins crisscrossing it.

At porch level, Em stood far above the lawman. She unwound her fists, making a conscious effort to look at ease.

"If you know his whereabouts," he went on, "you'd do him a favor by tellin' me. He'll get a fair trial."

Em could hear Chance's sarcastic voice answering, *Sure.*

"He didn't do it," Em managed to croak. "He's been minin' silver for over a year. Them nuggets was his."

The sheriff barked, "He's the only black man for twenty miles, and he left a trail a fresh fish could follow. It made a beeline for the Rocking H."

"He didn't do it, Mr. Sheriff," Em repeated. "That's all I can tell you."

Feiklin eyed her, cold suspicion drawing up his lips. "I've got a posse scouring the hills. If they find him before he turns himself in, they may just have to shoot him for resisting arrest. I'm puttin' a five hundred dollar ree-ward out for the thief. Dead or alive."

Em clenched her teeth. She didn't make another sound.

Her tormentor pinned her under a killing stare for a count of ten before grabbing the trailing reins of his roan and heaving his bulk into the leather. "You think it over. I'll be back."

Weak as a newborn kitten, Em stepped inside and closed the door. She sank to the settee, bowed her head on her hands, and sobbed.

❧

Unaware of Em's despair, Wyatt and Banjo enjoyed a pleasant ride. Though afternoon, the air still held that gentle nip, that subtle coolness craved by mountain folk and city dwellers alike. Summer had finally cashed in her chips.

Banjo resettled his ragged hat and glanced at his companion mounted on the handsome honey-colored horse with satiny white mane and tail. "What do ya think?" he asked.

"About Chance?" Wyatt replied. "He's innocent, Banjo. I knew that before I left the house this morning."

"That's what I figured, too. I wish Feiklin wasn't so quick on the trigger."

"I tried to tell him," Wyatt said, "but he wasn't havin' any."

In Juniper, they tied their mounts to the hitching rail in front of the tiny stage station. Except for a plump housewife walking down the boardwalk with a basket on her arm, the town looked dead.

Inside the station, the men removed their hats and glanced around. They smelled raw tobacco. The stage depot measured half the size of Harper's store. A short backless bench lay tucked against the right wall as they entered. To the left hung a cork board covered with a schedule, various notices, and a freshly printed wanted poster. The men paused to read it: "$500 reward for the man who robbed the Cedar Grove stage." It didn't mention Chance by name. Four strides from the door sat a man behind the counter, a short, leathery gent with a handlebar mustache and a scar on his left jaw. The black mustache twitched into a smile when he saw Banjo.

"Well, howdy, Banjo, you ole sidewinder. I haven't seen you in a coon's age. . .Wyatt. How's it goin'?"

Wyatt nodded a greeting.

"We've been gettin' in the corn crop and reddin' up the place for winter," Banjo said, his manner relaxed and friendly, "so I haven't been in town for a while. I hear you've had some excitement hereabouts." He leaned an arm on the polished walnut surface between him and Buckeye Mullins.

"Don't you know it." The mustache drooped back into place and Mullins shifted a wad of Bull Durham tobacco to the other side of his mouth. "First time one of my stages has been hit. I'd like to tie the thievin' hairpin to the nearest tree."

"Any idea who did it?" Banjo probed.

"Black man, six foot tall (give or take an inch), medium

build. He wasn't wearing a mask. He rode a tall bay with a white blaze."

Not good. Po'boy was a tall bay with a white blaze.

"What did the hombre look like?"

"Look like?" the stage manager barked. "What does it matter? They all look alike. Ain't that many black boys in these parts." He squinted at Wyatt. "Matter of fact, your cook is the only one I know of."

Wyatt's lips tightened.

Banjo quickly asked, "Who was on the stage, Buckeye? Anyone I know?"

Mullins grasped a giant black ledger and pulled it toward him. Flipping it open, he ran a wide finger down the page. "Byron Cotton had a ticket through to Colorado Springs. And A.J. Kinny of Cedar Grove." He closed the book. "Just them two. The driver, Shorty Gates, drives through to Colorado Springs. He'll be back tomorrow night."

They chatted a few minutes about the frightening increase in crime before Wyatt and Banjo broke away and stepped back into the sunshine.

"I know Kinny, one of the passengers," Banjo told his friend. "He works in a blacksmith shop fixin' pots and coffee grinders. Let's ride to Cedar Grove and have a little talk with him."

Wyatt nodded. "We can check out the site of the robbery when we pass it. But first, let's cross over to the livery stable. I'd like to hear what Link Hensler has to say for himself."

Across Main Street and two places north, Benson's livery was owned by a man with the girth of a fifty-gallon drum. He spent his days in a chair beside the wide double doors. Whether he sat inside or outside depended on the weather, but he always occupied his place. Benson found it easiest to hire passing saddle bums and youngsters to muck out the stalls and dole out grain.

Today, the doors stood wide, the sun reaching far inside to chase away the morning's chill. Banjo paused only long enough to say, "Hensler around?"

Benson jerked his meaty head to the left. "He's on shovel duty inside. Help yourself."

The stable reeked of manure, hay, and horseflesh. Only three residents filled the ten slots lining the back of the wide room: a bay, a paint, and a buckskin.

Wyatt cast an appraising eye over the horses. "That's Hensler's horse," he told Banjo in low tones, indicating the buckskin. Pausing a brief moment, the men took in the long deep ridges streaking the horse's belly and sides. Wyatt's jaw hardened. Evidently Hensler frequently gouged spurs to his mount, a practice that Wyatt, a former wrangler, despised.

"Ya lookin' for something?" Hensler's drawl sounded out from the end of the building.

"Howdy, Hensler," Wyatt called. "We came to ask you about Saturday." He led the way toward the hostler.

Hensler leaned a grubby shirt sleeve on a spade handle, dark eyes on his callers.

"When you came on Chance in Juniper, I mean," the blond man finished. "What exactly happened?"

Banjo sized up the man while Wyatt talked. Five foot eleven and one hundred sixty pounds, Link Hensler had a thin, flat frame that matched his flat face. His thick red lips pursed as he considered Wyatt's question. Was that suspicion lurking behind his eyes?

The hostler waited a moment before answering, "The sheriff and Buckeye Mullins had told a bunch of us at the restaurant how a black man had robbed the stage. Well, you and I both know they's only one hombre in these parts who fits that description." He scratched his belly with broken, black nails. "Me and some fellows—Tom, Jim, Joey, and Abe—were moseying down the street on Saturday just mindin' our business when that black boy stepped out of Harper's holdin' a new shovel. Well, we all looked at each other and someone said, 'Let's take him. He ain't heeled.'

"So we all cat-footed up behind him. He saw us before we could grab him, and all of a sudden he turned into a wild man. Knocked Jim and Tom down and cut open Abe's head. The thievin' galoot jumped into the saddle and lit out like the devil himself was on his tail." Hensler shrugged. "That's the last we saw of him."

Banjo spoke, "Did anyone mention hangin' him?"

Hensler's grin had a wicked curve. "Now that you ask, I reckon someone did. But nothin' came of it. He got plumb away before we could lay hands on a rope."

Noting Wyatt's set look, his tight fist, Banjo said, "We'd best be headin' out, Wyatt." He caught the young rancher's eye. "We've got some ridin' to do."

He turned to the hostler. "Thanks for the chin music, Hensler. We heard Chance had been in town, and we wanted to hear about it."

"There's a posse out today," the shovel-wielding man volunteered, "but I couldn't go. I hope they get him quick. He deserves to get his neck stretched. A body won't feel safe till he's behind bars at least." He leaned over, thrusting the blunt end of the spade along the ground.

Five minutes later, donkey and horse cantered out of town, humble Kelsey keeping time with elegant Ben. Slowing to a walk as a grove of pines and scrub oaks closed around them, Banjo leaned forward, studying the ground.

"The trail's a day old already, but we haven't had any rain. We should still be able to find. . ." He drew up on the reins. "Eureka!" Quickly, he swung down. Wyatt followed suit but stood well back, his eyes on the soil at Banjo's feet.

eleven

Banjo squatted beside the road, pointing. "Here's the stage tracks. They have narrow wheels, too fine for a buckboard. Yesterday's stage cut through them. The horses must have been nervous during the holdup because the wheels of this coach rocked back and forth a few times. See it?"

"I'm following ya."

"There's a nice boot print on the side. Must be the driver's. The thief stayed mounted." He moved off the trail into softer earth. "Here's some horse tracks." Wyatt circled around to join Banjo without stepping on the marks in the dirt.

"Those aren't Rocking H shoes," the young rancher declared. "They're too heavy. Slim uses a lighter shoe. He does all our smithing."

Banjo glanced at the sun, glowing high in the sky. "We have a little time. Let's see where he went."

They quartered the roadside, searching for a trail away from the robbery. Fifteen minutes later, Wyatt raised his hand. "Over here! He cut away south then turned back north into our land." He squinted at the sky, figuring the direction. "He headed straight for the ranch if he stayed on course."

They wound through the trees, studying the ground, before mounting up and quickening the pace. A quarter of a mile later, a small stream cut across their path. The muddy edge was trampled, a mixture of boot prints and horseshoes.

"Well, looky here," Banjo said, stepping down. He peered

at the tracks, memorizing the details. "He has a bit of a drag on the left leg. Probably not noticeable to someone watching him walk."

Wyatt scanned the opposite bank. "He crossed over. Still headed for the ranch." He stroked his beard. "Why would he come to the Rocking H? He ought to be running for the hills."

"Feiklin has seen these same tracks, Hammond. No wonder he thinks Chance is guilty. Our good sheriff has quite a case." Banjo stared at the tracks across the stream, lips pursed. "I think somebody's runnin' a blazer, deliberately pointing to Chance."

"What a lowdown trick!" Wyatt wasn't surprised that they might be up against a con artist's hoax, but it didn't increase their odds of catching the villain.

Banjo's features hardened. "We're gonna nail his hide, Hammond. I'm promisin' you that." He picked up Kelsey's dragging reins. "Let's go."

The thief's trail led through the yard of a dilapidated line shack with a sagging roof and straight into the Rocking H yard. He'd tethered his horse to the hitching rail beside the bunkhouse. Scouring the ground, Wyatt found several older tracks nearby. Evidently, the guilty man frequently visited the Rocking H.

Or maybe he worked there.

Wyatt pulled off his brown, flat-crowned hat and scratched his head. "Let's say howdy to Susan and get a drink before we move along."

Banjo rubbed his stomach and said, "I'm agreeable. Maybe she's been baking pies or bear sign."

Wyatt chuckled at Banjo's use of that name for doughnuts. "After this morning, she'd probably throw them at me."

The men walked around the house to enter through the back. Giving Banjo a watch-this expression, Wyatt eased the kitchen door open twelve inches. "Should I throw my hat in first?" he called.

Susan's saucy voice came back, "Wyatt Hammond, what are you up to now?" Her slender hand pushed the door open; her slim form filled the doorway. She ran lightly toward Wyatt, aimed for his arms. Catching sight of Banjo at the last minute, she drew up short, cheeks flaming. "Banjo! How nice to see you!"

Banjo's stubbled jaw widened into a grin. "We thought we'd wet our whistles while we're close."

Wyatt slipped his arm about his wife's waist, laughing eyes looking down at her. "A sandwich or two would hit the spot. We may not be back till late."

"Welcome to my parlor," Susan laughed, stepping back to let them in. "I've got two steaks in the frying pan. You caught me cooking lunch. The beans are already finished."

"If you weren't already employed, I'd hire you," Wyatt teased, tweaking her ponytail as she hurried away. The men found seats at the kitchen table.

"Did you find Chance?" Susan asked, forking mansize steaks onto plates.

"He's safe," her husband said. "We talked to him."

"Come on, Wyatt," she urged, "don't quit now. What did he say?" She dished up beans and set the food before them. Grabbing two cups, she poured coffee.

Wyatt quickly told her of Chance's silver mine and Banjo's theory that someone had framed the cook. "We're on our way to Cedar Grove to talk to one of the stage passengers who saw the thief," he finished.

Chewing a juicy bit of beef, Banjo noted that Wyatt hadn't mentioned the trail that led to their ranch. Swallowing the last of their coffee, they reached for their hats.

"Thanks for the meal, Miss Susan," Banjo said. "It's good to see you lookin' so fit."

Susan's bantering mood faded. Absolutely serious, she gazed from Banjo to Wyatt and back again. "Help Chance, Banjo," she said. "For Em's sake. Help him."

"We're givin' it a brass-plated try," Banjo replied.

"Don't worry if I'm late," Wyatt said, planting his hat above his ears.

They rode into Cedar Grove as the light faded to dull gloom. At the northern edge of town, the blacksmith shop had its doors locked. Closed for the day.

"There's a light on at the sheriff's office," Banjo said, prodding Kelsey forward. "He'll know where Kinny lives."

Following the white-haired lawman's terse directions, they stumbled up the dark stairs outside the general store. The moon had not yet risen, and they didn't have a lantern. Kinny lived in an apartment above the store.

Banjo knocked loudly, calling, "A.J. Kinny? It's me, Banjo Calahan."

The door creaked inward. From the semidark interior a scratchy, deep voice boomed, "What're you doin' in this neck o' the woods, Banjo, you old hooligan? Come on in. Who's yer partner?"

The tall man with his hand on the door was bacon thin, with the stooped shoulders of a man who'd spent years bending over a worktable. His ruddy face looked like a rubber ball squeezed in the middle so that the top bulged up. His forehead stretched more than four inches from deep-set eyes to a close-cropped shock of brown hair.

Banjo stepped across the sill. "Meet Wyatt Hammond, owner of the Rocking H spread. This is A.J. Kinny. We used to work together on the Lazy R." He playfully punched Kinny's chest. "That was at least a century ago, eh, A.J.?"

"Maybe two from the looks of you." Kinny haw-hawed. He stretched a big bony hand toward the table and chairs in the center of the room. "Light and set."

Each chose a straight-backed chair around the yellow glow of a single lantern in the center of the square table. The room was clean but spare. No curtains. No rugs. No woman's touch.

Banjo got right to the point. "You were on the stage that got robbed Friday night."

"For my sins." Kinny's unsightly mug waited expectantly.

"The sheriff of Juniper thinks a friend of ours held up that stage, A.J. We need to know exactly what the robber looked like. It could mean an innocent man's freedom."

"He was a black man on a tall bay."

Banjo glanced at Wyatt and waited. When Kinny didn't volunteer more details, Banjo's eyes bored into the lean man. "Surely you can tell us more than that. What was his hair like? Did he wear a mask? How tall was he? What build? What about his clothes? Did he have a gun?"

Kinny held up a hand as though warding off a blow. "Okay. Okay. I've got you in my sights." He coughed and shifted in the chair, making it creak. With hair like that, he might have just stepped in from a gale. Each short brown strand stood on end, but few went in the same direction.

The gangly man cocked his head, remembering. "We'd been in the stage for about an hour when a shout made me and Cotton look out. Cotton was the other passenger.

"The coach drew up real quick like. Outside beside the driver was this black man mounted on a bay and wavin' a hogleg like he meant it. I heard him say, 'Hand me the strongbox and no funny business.'"

Banjo interrupted. "What was his voice like?"

Squinting, Kinny paused. "He sounded like a gent from Dixie. Took twice as long to get those words out as you or I would."

Banjo leaned a forearm on the table, concentrating on the man's words.

"His hair touched his shoulders. It was coal black and woolly comin' out from under his Stetson. Looked like he forgot how to use a comb.

"Once he'd set the strongbox in his lap, he prodded his horse over to the door of the stage and told us to hand out our cash."

"What about his skin?" Banjo prompted. "How dark was it?"

"When I said black I meant it. Now that I think about it, he looked a little strange, that black face with fat red lips. Night was coming on, and his lips was about all I could see in the bad light. I remember thinkin' how shiny my gold eagles looked in his coal-black palm."

"What kind of gun?"

"A Colt, I guess." He paused. "No, wait a minute. It was a pepperbox, a twelve shot." He grinned but without humor. "That bore looked big as a cannon pointin' my way." His rough voice became tense, impatient. "Anything else you want to know?"

"Think back real close," Banjo said. "Did you see any marks on him? Anything besides his skin color that would set him apart?"

Kinny relaxed in the hard chair, eyes gazing dully into a dark corner. His visitors didn't move a muscle. Silently they willed him to recall some vital tidbit that would buy Chance's freedom.

Suddenly, Kinny's face took on a surprised look. "Yes, by

jingo," he said. "A jagged scar on the back of his gun hand, his right. It's an ugly thing. Raised and bumpy."

Banjo thumped the table with his fist. "That's the ticket."

Kinny's good humor reappeared. "Now that you've pumped me dry, would you like some coffee?" Banjo shoved his chair away from the table and stood. Wyatt followed suit.

"Wish we had time, A.J.," the old-timer said, settling his stained Stetson in place. "But we've got to mosey along." He shook the blacksmith's carbon-stained hand. "We'll have to get together and swap yarns sometime. I owe you one, A.J. Call on me anytime."

"I'll do it." Kinny followed them to the door and shut the travelers into the night.

The journey home seemed double long as the hour approached midnight. "Rock of Ages. . ." Banjo's low voice drifted on the breeze.

When he tired of singing, wild night sounds closed about the riders. Banjo yawned. "If I'd brought my blanket roll, I'd sleep under the stars tonight. I'm plumb tuckered out. Maybe I should fix myself a Scotch hammock."

"What's that?"

"They're easy to make." The puncher pulled Kelsey closer to Ben to make talking easier. "First, you find two trees about six feet apart. Ya nail the south end of your longjohns to one tree, then ya stretch yourself over and nail the north end to the other'n." Hammond's long, echoing laughter ricocheted from boulders and rocky hills. Banjo's sandpaper voice joined him.

Wyatt waved a good-bye and split off when Rocking H range met the trail, leaving Banjo to his own thoughts until he reached the Circle C.

Kinny's description of the thief didn't come close to matching the light-skinned cook. Why hadn't someone thought of that before?

twelve

Em woke to brilliant sunshine the next morning. In spite of the light, to her the day had a dreary cast from the moment she opened her eyes. She performed a hasty toilet, shrugged into yesterday's work dress, and trod to the kitchen.

What had Banjo learned in Cedar Grove? Why had he come back so late? She'd waited up until past ten. Weary and utterly discouraged, she'd turned in only to toss for two more hours.

Her thoughts wandered to Chance, cold and hungry in that dark hole. *Please, God,* she prayed, *bring him safely home and safely to You.*

Fumbling flour into the mixing bowl, she dropped the scoop on the floor. White powder covered her dress, the cabinet front, and the floor. Em stared at the mess, thoroughly disgusted.

"What'sa matter, Em?" Jeremy's shrill voice startled her.

"I'm all thumbs and elbows this morning, Jeremy," Em retorted. "Now look what I've done."

"I'll help you." The child ran for a damp dishcloth.

Em took it from his hand. "Thank ye, child, I'll be needin' a broom, too." She dabbed at her skirt while Jeremy skittered to the back door.

Despite the accident, breakfast was a tasty treat delivered on time. Steve greeted Em with the words, "Megan had a bad night. She's sleeping now and I didn't want to wake her."

Steve and Banjo piled biscuits and bacon on their plates,

covering the whole with Em's salty milk gravy. At the far end of the table, Jeremy finished his third biscuit with sorghum. Before him was a half-empty glass of Bess's milk. Eyes wide, he listened to the men talk.

"How was huntin' yesterday, Banjo?" Steve asked after he'd tasted his coffee.

Bit by bit, Banjo relayed the many events of his travels. "I feel certain some palooka's trying to buffalo the law," he concluded. "If Chance was guilty, he'd have covered his tracks. The jasper didn't even wear a mask, for pity's sake."

Across from Banjo, Em's plate was still clean. "Feiklin rode in after you left," she announced, listlessly, sipping black coffee. In two sentences she described the sheriff's words and attitude. "I didn't tell him anything, but I feel certain sure he'll be back." She turned haunted eyes toward Steve. "What'll I say, Mr. Steve?"

"You'll have to tell the truth if he keeps after you." He took in Em's unwilling frown. "You'll have to tell Chance to go someplace else and not tell you where. That's the only way I can figure it."

Banjo added, "If we knew he'd get an honest trial, there'd be no problem. But with Hensler puttin' fuel to the fire every time he can, I'm afraid the townsfolk will be dressin' Chance in a California collar." He used a scrap of biscuit to mop up the last drops of gravy.

In a moment he went on, "Kinny said the thief had coal black skin. That lets Chance out by a country mile. The robber rode a horse that wasn't shod at the Rocking H. Wyatt confirmed that. Another thing, the holdup man talked with a slow southern drawl. Chance comes from Georgia, but he talks like a lawyer from Philadelphia." Banjo grinned at Em. "He's right uncanny, is your Chance."

Em straightened. "*My* Chance?"

Ignoring her, Banjo said, "Let me see your hand."

Studying his face, Em stretched out her fingers, palm up.

Steve watched the interchange closely, curiosity openly displayed on his features. Banjo nodded. "That's what I figured."

"What is it?" Steve demanded.

"Her palm is tan, not much darker than mine." He laid his own calloused hand next to Em's slim one. "Kinny said his gold eagles glowed against the thief's black palm." He leaned forward excitedly. "That proves the thief wasn't really a black man. He was a white man runnin' a blazer, trying to make out like he was black to bring the law on Chance."

Em's waning strength drained away, leaving her limp. "Who would do such a devilish thing?" she whispered, horrified.

His lips tightened. "That's what I aim to find out. As soon as I can figure out how." He paused at Em's disheartened sigh. "Now, Em, when trouble comes, there's three things you can do: go to pieces, go to drinkin', or go to God. The first two don't accomplish much, so let's take hold of the third."

The anxious woman managed a weak smile. "I'se a-tryin', Banjo."

He relaxed, glancing at Steve. "What's on the work list for today?"

Steve set down his cup. "I figure we need to get some logs split and stacked. Jeremy and I hauled in three loads of wood yesterday. One of deadfall and two more from the trees I cut last week."

All heads swiveled east as the bedroom door creaked open. Deep circles under her eyes, Megan waddled toward the table. "I don't want to scare anyone," she said, "but I've been having pains every eight minutes for the last half hour."

Steve bounded from his chair to take her arm. He led her to

the table and pulled out a chair at the corner between his seat and Em's.

"You feelin' hungry?" Em asked.

"Only thirsty," Megan replied weakly. "I'd like some cold water."

At Steve's nod, Jeremy left his chair to fetch a clean glass and head for the spring.

"I'll get the maul and start on that wood," Banjo said, rising. He tramped outside, boots thudding against the wood floor. Jeremy set a glass of water before Megan and ran after him.

"Are the pains bad?" Em asked. She touched Megan's cool forehead and smoothed back her hair.

"Not really painful, just uncomfortable. I was having them last night. That's why I couldn't sleep."

"I'll make you some tea, and then it's back to bed with you, little lady," Em announced. She turned to Steve, hovering anxiously nearby. "It ain't the real thing yet. Just a practice run." She placed a loving arm around Megan's shoulders. "But it's a good sign we won't have too much longer to wait."

Megan lay her head on Em's shoulder. "I wish it were over already. I'm so tired. Every day is so long."

After settling Megan comfortably, Em went through her chores with automatic hands. She ran Banjo's news through her mind, wondering who could be so evil as to try to hurt honest Chance.

Later in the day Megan stepped out to the spring where Em bent over a scrub board. "I feel much, much better, Em," she said, smiling. "Steve finished the cradle last night. I think I'll stuff the mattress for it this afternoon. That is, after I find something to eat. I'm starving."

The sight of her happy face brought Em a surge of energy.

"That's fine, Miss Megan. The ticking is in the sideboard drawer. I cut it out last night." She slapped the cloth in her hands. Suds flew up. "I'll be done here in a little while."

Megan disappeared inside as Em attacked the soiled bedsheet. The new arrival would certainly be soon. Megan had started feathering her nest.

❧

The next morning, Em packed a basket with jerky, canned peaches, sandwiches, biscuits, and a covered dish of hot stew. Banjo carried the food out to the buckboard while Em fetched two wool blankets. The sun had hardly cleared the horizon when they pulled away from the house. Oatmeal and biscuits sat hot and ready on the back of the stove for the Chamberlin family to help themselves when they roused. Em and Banjo were on their way to visit Chance.

"Have you thought up any new ideas for smokin' out that lying robber?" Em asked.

"Been beatin' my brains to a pulp," he answered, shaking his head regretfully. "Maybe talkin' to Chance will give me some fresh ammunition."

"Somethin's gotta happen soon. I'se afraid Sheriff Feiklin will come on Chance in that cave."

"Just you remember," Banjo warned, "the good Lord sees Chance. He knows all about this trouble."

"Sometimes I get so tied up, I can't remember anything except that poor man hidin' in a dark hole, afraid for his life."

"We've got to pray that hombre into the kingdom." The force of Banjo's words brought a questioning look from the woman beside him. "You've got a bad case of Cupid's cramps, Em. Like it or not. The only answer is to pray a certain dark gentleman into the family of God."

With a sudden absurd impulse to give way to tears, Em stared straight ahead. She didn't say another word until they reached Fox Hole Creek.

Chance stood waiting in the door of the cave when they arrived. His face was gaunt, his eyes sunken. Em thrust the basket into his hands and followed him inside, Banjo trailing close behind with blankets tucked under his arm.

"Has anyone come around here?" Em asked anxiously as Chance plopped to the floor and dug into the basket.

Shaking his head in answer to her question, he lifted out the bowl of stew. "Pardon me, Emma. As Amos says, I'm as hungry as a woodpecker with a headache." He dove into the beef and potatoes.

Banjo placed the blankets on the rumpled coat beside the cave wall. The wheelbarrow and tools sat in a new place. Dirt crusted the pick and shovel.

"Sheriff Feiklin has a posse combin' the hills for you," Banjo said. "He tried to get Em to tell him where you are."

Em added, "I didn't tell him nothin', but I'm afraid he'll come again." She paused. "I can't lie to him, Chance."

The starving man finished the last bite of beef and reached into the basket for a sandwich. "I haven't seen anyone." He got his mouth around the first sandwich, chewed, and swallowed. "They got a reward out for me?"

Em nodded sadly. "Five hundred dollars." She stood in front of Chance so she could watch his expression.

He stopped chewing to stare hard at Banjo. His jaws moved twice more before he swallowed. "Why didn't you turn me in? That's a fair amount of money."

"I wish you'd believe we want to help you," Banjo said, sitting down near him.

Puzzled, Chance eyed the man beside him a moment longer

before chomping down more bread and meat.

"Wyatt and I did some scoutin' where the robbery happened," Banjo continued. "And we talked to a man who was sittin' in the stage." He related Kinny's account. "The way I see it, a white man got himself up to look like a black man. He left a trail a mile wide heading straight back to the Rocking H. It was a put-up job."

Chance's expression changed from watchfulness to sullen calculation. He said, "There's more than one man on the Rocking H who's onery enough to do that to me. Jack Savage lives to put me down. Doesn't he, Em?"

"He's right, Banjo," Em confirmed. "I'se seen him ride Chance more than once."

"The thief had thick, black hair reaching to his shoulders," Banjo said, slowly. "That matches at least."

"The three musketeers aren't above it either," the accused man added. "They've been in more than one scrape since they came around. Gambling. Chasing calico. Guzzling whiskey. You name it."

Banjo knocked the tattered Stetson to the back of his head. "I've been studyin' on it till my head aches. Somehow we've got to smoke the thievin' galoot into the open."

"What did he do with the strongbox?" Chance asked, wiping his hands on dusty pant legs. "It must be somewhere around the ranch."

Banjo scratched his days-old stubble, considering. "You might have something there. The strongbox must weigh a good thirty pounds. Set in front of him like that, it wouldn't ride easy. Either he dumped it someplace along the way or he took it to the ranch and hid it there. He wouldn't carry it anywhere folks would see it, that's sure."

Em picked up the basket and unpacked the rest of the food

items, placing them on a new shelf Chance had carved from the hard earth wall.

Banjo stood. "I'll ride over the thief's trail again today. Who knows? I may find something else this time. It's happened before." He glanced at Em. "I'll mosey on down to the wagon, Em. You come when you're ready." He ambled out the small opening and disappeared.

Chance got to his feet and came near Em. "For the first time, I can see why you like him, Emma."

"He's a Christian, Chance. A real Christian looks beyond the color of a man's skin. Jesus died for us all, you know."

He smirked. "You sermonizing at me again?"

The worry mark deepened. "I can't help preachin' sometimes!" she exclaimed. "Jesus can set you free like no man or no man's law can ever do. I wish you could believe that."

He grimaced. "Freedom?" He walked a step beyond her. His next words came from over his shoulder as he stared at the inky back of the cave. "We laughed and shouted and danced back in sixty-five, out of our minds with joy because we'd been set free. What foolish children we were!" He jerked around to face her. His eyes were glowing coals. "Now I know a black man can never be free. Not really free like other folks are."

"Chance. . ." She touched his sleeve.

He shook her off. "Save it, Emma!" A second later, his face softened. "Forgive me. I didn't mean to shout at you. I just can't abide any more preaching." He dug into his pocket for a match.

"I've been busy since you came last time." He picked up the bachelor's lantern and the match flared to life. "Come with me."

Light held high, he led her toward the mine shaft. Only,

now the tunnel was no more than six feet deep. Em leaned forward, peering closely at the mound of loose dirt that reached within two feet of the ceiling.

"It's a false wall," he explained. "I dug out the back of the shaft and piled the dirt here. If anyone does find me, I'll crawl in here. . ." Stooping, he set down the lantern to tug at a knee-high stone. Splotchy brown, it was pitted and rough. "This looks heavier than it is. It's limestone. I found it in a pile near the creek last night and rolled it up here." With a little effort the rock came out of the hole in the dirt wall. Behind it, Em could see a cavity.

"What's that? A little tunnel?" She squatted beside him.

"It's a big hollow log." He moved the candle flame closer. "I mean, it's hollow at this end. The top end is two feet thick.

"I've been scouring the country just before dawn and at the edge of dark, looking for something to make me a hidey-hole. I spent two hours brushing out the track from dragging this piece of cottonwood up here." He pointed upward inside the hole. "It goes up about four feet. If I squeeze, I can get in there and pull the stone after me."

"Chance! You'll stifle in there!" Em's face mirrored her alarm.

"You're good at praying," he replied. "So, pray I won't have to use it." He got to his feet.

Em stood also. "I best be goin'," she said. "I'll be back day after tomorrow." She paused. "I know you put a lot of sweat into that little place, but you really ought to find another cave or something. Someplace I don't know about." Her voice caught, then she plunged on. "I can't lie for you, Chance. Much as I want to help you, I can't lie." She snatched up the empty basket and headed out the door.

Stumbling ahead, she blinked away hot tears. When she

reached the wagon, her cheeks were dry but she was still weeping in her heart.

Banjo was lounging in the buckboard when she arrived. He helped her aboard and shook the reins. The horses, Billy and Star, jolted into motion.

The sun slid beneath a billowing gray cloud. When they reached their own creek bed, the first smattering drops hit Em's hand. The brown hides on their horses became splotched as the rain increased.

Shading her eyes, she looked up. It seemed all nature wept with her.

thirteen

Splitting wood under an oak on the east side of the house, Wyatt didn't act surprised when Banjo rode into his yard in time for lunch that same day. The shower had passed, leaving in its wake a clean, sharp smell. Hammond lowered the ax long enough to raise a wide hand in greeting.

"I see you under that Stetson, Banjo. You caught me chorin' like a sodbuster. Chance usually splits the kitchen wood." He thunked the ax into the much-scored stump acting as a chopping base. "What's up?"

Wearing a rain slicker and slouching in the saddle, Banjo told him about his visit to Chance that morning. "We've got to find that strongbox, Wyatt. It must be stashed around here somewhere."

"Around here?" Wyatt repeated, scanning the circle of buildings before him. He stroked his beard, lips pursed. "You do have a point. He must have ditched it soon after he left the stage." Bending to fill his arms with wood, he said, "I'll take these in for Susan. We'll take a gander around the bunkhouse while the hands are settin' up to the table."

Banjo tied Kelsey to the rail beside the bunkhouse. He pulled off the slicker, tied it behind the cantle, and strode into the left stable. He looked down the line of horses: Susan's chestnut gelding, Wyatt's palomino, two roans, and two duns. He strolled to the next stable and counted three buckskins, four duns, and a paint. Ten horses wandered about the box-shaped corral spreading behind the stables and up one side of the yard. Not a single bay in Hammond's remuda. Unless one worked on the range.

When Wyatt joined him at the corral fence, Banjo asked, "You got any bays in your string?"

"Yeah, a small mare. She's combin' the brakes with Slim today."

Banjo pulled off his John B. and scratched his head. "I wonder where the thief got his horse. It was a tall bay with a blaze, like Po'boy."

"This thing's gettin' downright spooky," Wyatt declared. He glanced toward the house where the hands were eating. "Let's take a look in the bunkhouse while we can." He led the way. The hands' quarters ran at right angles to the west of the stables. Hammond pushed open the door and stepped inside.

Built like a railroad car, the doghouse—as the hands called it—contained ten sets of bunks in close regimentation. More than half of these were unoccupied at this slack time of year. The beds were in varying degrees of disorder. In the front area stood a blackened stove, a table of rough lumber, and six chairs. A lantern and a disheveled checker game graced the tabletop. Assorted clothes and bits of tack hung from nails on the walls.

Wyatt knelt to look under beds while Banjo moved along feeling wool blankets and hanging clothes. Beside the back door at the opposite end of the building stood a small table with a pitcher and basin. A roll towel hung above it. Nothing there.

Banjo scanned the ground along the wooden structure, seeking freshly dug earth. Nothing there either.

Wyatt's scuffling boots announced his arrival. He swung open the back door and stepped out. "Looks like we've struck out here," he said. "Want to try the haymow?"

Banjo nodded. "That's as good an idea as any, I reckon."

Fifteen minutes of concentrated searching yielded no results. Back at the woodpile, Wyatt pried the ax away from the stump and sat down where it had been. He said, "So much for that bit of genius. He must have dumped off the box before he got here."

"Let's ride back the way he came," Banjo suggested. "The tracks are long gone by now, but we know his trail. If he buried the box, we should be able to see where."

"I'll saddle Ben," Hammond said and strode away.

Banjo claimed Wyatt's empty seat and snatched a brown grass straw to chew on. Suddenly, the porch door slammed back and the hands poured out.

"Hey, you old souwegian!" Curly belted out when he reached the woodpile.

"Howdy, Curly," Banjo replied, chuckling. "How's life treatin' you?"

The foreman replied, "Not bad if a body don't mind chasin' cantankerous cow young'uns out of the brush. That's where we're headed now."

"You takin' Cavenaugh along?" Banjo joked. "By the looks of him I'd say he's headed for a church social."

Jake's laughter shook the trees.

Brent pulled out his most winning grin and said, "Everybody couldn't be handsome, so God picked out just us few."

"Now, Brent," Amos drawled, "you know I'm just as good-lookin' as you."

That brought a hoot from everyone and the hands moved on. Curly paused a moment longer than the rest.

"One good thing about Cavenaugh," Banjo told the foreman, "he's hardly ever talking about other folks."

Curly grinned. "Take care of yourself, old-timer," he said and moved away.

Halfway across the yard, the bald foreman met Wyatt with Ben's reins in his grip. They stopped for a word. Banjo fetched Kelsey.

Hammond and Banjo rode past the hitching rail and into the trees. Brown leaves and pine needles littered the ground, making their quest more difficult. Once out of sight of the ranch, they slowed to a crawl, eyes on the ground. Twice Banjo dismounted for a closer look, then mounted again and moved on.

At the old line shack they dropped their reins and scouted around the rickety building. The house seemed boarded shut, but on closer inspection, the board over the door was only propped in place.

Banjo tugged at it. The wood came off easily in his hands. "Well, looky here," he drawled. "Somebody's been in here. And not long ago."

Wyatt peered through the door. "Let's take a gander inside." The interior of the house was much like the bunkhouse, small and bare with two sets of bunks, one on each side, and a fireplace covering most of the back wall. Musty odors clogged their noses. Banjo peered overhead. The roof showed spots of sky at irregular intervals.

An iron grate and pot hovered over the dead fire, testifying to a thousand meals eaten and forgotten. In the center of the room, two benches formed a V before the hearth, a small stool that doubled as a table at the apex.

Peering under beds, running hands over the rotting straw mattresses, the men scoured the room. Banjo stirred a half-burned stick around the inside of the cooking pot and Wyatt tapped the mud chinking.

On the thick mantel shelf resided a lantern, a large rusty

can, and a tin of matches. Wyatt lifted the can and reached inside. He pulled out a cloth bundle and took it to the door for better light.

"What do you know about this?" He held the open cloth toward his partner. On his palm lay a stump of burnt cork, a bag of white lime, and a homemade horsehair brush. "That's not all," Wyatt announced, handing the items to Banjo.

He reached into the can again and pulled out a wad of black fibers. Shaking the packet loose, it became a black woolly wig.

"Great sand and sagebrush!" Banjo exclaimed. He stepped back and found a seat on the nearest bench. "What do you make of that?"

"Our man stopped here long enough to hide his costume," Wyatt said. "Burnt cork to black his face, a wig to hide his own hair. . . See that lime? If he mixed it with a little water, he could use it to paint a blaze on his horse. He made himself a little brush to do it with." Banjo held the horsehair brush aloft before handing it back to Wyatt. The rancher stuffed the objects back into the can. "He must have hid the money here, too."

"Wyatt," Banjo said, suddenly, "say we do find the money. How will we know who buried it?"

The blond bearded gent stared at the can in his hands, considering.

"We can quit lookin'," Banjo announced, excitement in his voice. "If we draw the hairpin out of hidin', he'll lead us to the money and nail himself at the same time."

"Keep talkin'," Wyatt invited.

Head cocked, inner wheels turning, the veteran leaned forward and spoke in low tones.

❧

An hour after Em left him, Chance hunkered down near the

mouth of his cave, ears straining. The clink of a horseshoe on stone had fine tuned his senses to an excruciating pitch. He peered through a thin spot in the dry brush piled before the entrance. Fine misty rain clouded the air.

Did friend or foe lurk outside?

With frantic haste, he gathered the food Em had brought. Stuffing the jerky into his jeans pocket, he dropped the cans and biscuits on his blankets. Bundling them together, he threw the whole into the darkest corner of the room. He grabbed a handful of sticks from the brush at the doorway to scuff out his footprints as he backed up to the false wall. His heart was pounding so loudly he feared his pursuers would find him by its traitorous clangor alone. He crayfished into the hole and strained to roll the stone into the opening.

His knees nudged his chin. Dirt fell into his eyes.

How long could he endure the log's squeezing him? It had looked so wide before, but now he felt as if he sat in a vise.

Already his heaving lungs cried for more air.

Would someone come?

Pressing his eyes closed, willing his breathing to calm, he slowly counted to five hundred. Twice more to five hundred and he would move. He must.

Sweat trickled into his collar.

A skating stone made him lose count.

"Hey! What's this?" someone called. Scraping wood and snapping twigs.

The brush at the entrance, Chance thought.

"A cave!" Was that Feiklin's resonant voice?

"Shall we look around, Sheriff?" a high-pitched nasal voice asked.

"Looks empty," Feiklin stated. Boots crunched on the dirt

floor. "Relax, fellows. We may as well wait out the rain in here."

"Someone's been here," the shrill voice said. Chance tagged this one as Mousy and cursed him for his keen eyes when he said, "Look! A shelf and the lantern!"

"Someone's been minin'," a third husky voice offered. "See those tools in the wheelbarrow?"

Feiklin said, "Let me see them, Tom." A short pause. "This shovel's brand new. It's not even rusted."

Mousy exclaimed, "That black rascal had a new shovel with him. He used it against us outside Harper's. I had a headache for two days after he walloped me."

Chance swallowed convulsively and sank his head lower between his knees.

"Light the lantern," Feiklin commanded.

In a moment Tom announced, "A blanket roll. . .and food. Two cans of peaches. Fresh biscuits, too. Ummm. . .good ones."

"Find a squirrel?" asked a new man, unheard until now.

Feiklin answered, disgusted, "Looks like he's already taken to tall timber, Abe. You see any tracks outside?"

"Only to the creek and back here. I saw a wagon's tracks come up to the big cottonwood a few times in the last week. Someone might have taken him away."

"Look in the back of the cave, Tom," the sheriff ordered. "There may be another chamber. . . .And Tom. If you see him, haul iron. No sense givin' him the first shot."

Chance's breath left him as heavy boots grated close.

"Hey, Abe," Tom called, "hand me that shovel."

In a moment, Chance felt the jarring of the shovel on the dirt somewhere above his head. A shower of dust fell. The shovel struck twice more.

God, Chance prayed, *if You're really there, please make him stop. He'll bury me alive.* A sharp pain stabbed his chest. He fought off faintness.

More footsteps and Tom's voice called, "Nothing there, Sheriff." The words came more muffled than before but were still clearly audible.

"The rain's let up," Feiklin said. "Let's check further up and then we'll head home. I'm feelin' narrow at the equator. It's past noon." Feiklin's equator was anything but narrow.

"No sense wastin' these vittles," Tom said. "Want a can o' peaches, Jim?"

"Throw her here," Mousy answered.

The rustle of dry branches and fading footfalls told Chance that they had gone.

Every impulse told Chance to break free of the wooden shroud that crushed him like a giant python. He fought for control. He must think.

Had the posse really gone? Was someone waiting in the darkness, stalking him?

Despite numb limbs and aching lungs, he waited. He counted his heartbeats to five thousand and then waited some more. When he finally moved, his legs were dead. He shoved the stone away with the last strength in his trembling hands and crawled from his prison on elbows, dragging his nerveless feet.

Outside, he lay on his side gasping. Weak tears dripped to the ground.

God, he prayed again, *I don't know if what Em says is true or not. But one thing I do know. You're there.*

fourteen

Banjo and Wyatt carefully restored the line shack to its original appearance. They parted ways there, so Wyatt rode back to the ranch alone. In a thinking mood, he returned to the wood pile and split enough wood to last the week. The sun was at half mast when he filled his arms the final time and headed for the kitchen.

"You sure are ambitious," Susan commented wonderingly. She looked half her age, enveloped in a red gingham bib apron, her ponytail bobbing as she spoke. "I declare you haven't filled the woodbox all the way to the top since we've been married."

"Got any coffee?" her husband asked, dropping into a chair beside the table. "I'm powerful thirsty."

"One barefoot cup of coffee comin' up," Susan chimed, reaching for a tin cup. "Supper's almost ready." She picked up a dishtowel and folded it several times. Using the cloth to pad her hand, she lifted the dented blue coffeepot.

Wyatt sipped the strong, black brew and watched his wife's graceful movements around the kitchen. He couldn't have told which he enjoyed more—the brew or the view.

"I'll serve the hands tonight," he announced when Susan had filled a platter with steaks. Ignoring her dubious expression, he grabbed the plate and headed for the back porch.

The hands were in their usual places, jawing and joking. Their talk died when they caught sight of their waiter. Slim drawled, "Got yourself a new job, Boss?"

"I always fancied myself a dough puncher, Slim," Wyatt joshed. "I've just kept it well hid till now." He kidded and laughed at their banter, but his keen eyes stayed busy. Three trips to the kitchen, and his duties were through.

Wyatt stayed with Susan through the dishwashing routine, drying and stacking for her. He loved to watch her smile as she talked to him. The memory of those terrifying days of sickness still were fresh in his mind. Dishes done, they moved to the front porch to rock and chat till crickets and coyotes had taken over the still air.

" 'Bout time to turn in, don't you think?" Susan asked, stifling a yawn. "I have to be up by four to start breakfast."

"You go ahead." Wyatt stood and stretched. "I've got to ride out."

"At this time of night?" she asked, a fearful look appearing on her face.

"Come inside and I'll explain." Rising, he took her hand and walked with her into the house. In the privacy of their living room, he pulled her into his arms, enjoying the scent of her hair.

She submitted to a short kiss before demanding, "Where are you going at this hour?"

"Banjo and I have a plan to trap the stagecoach bandit." As her mouth opened to protest, he hurriedly said, "I'm sorry, sweetheart, but I have to go. You were the one who made me promise to help Chance, weren't you?"

"Yes. But I didn't expect you to go off and get yourself killed doing it."

"If I see any flying bullets, I'll duck." He kissed her again and left quickly before she could argue any more.

Stepping off the porch, he strode across the dark yard to the stable. Saddling Ben, he led the animal away from the bunkhouse to circle the yard and end up ten yards into the trees. Snubbing the stallion to a tree branch, he found his way back. Light from the three bunkhouse windows guided him the last few feet. Finding the latch by instinct, he stepped inside.

Hunched over the small table, Curly, Slim, Jake, and Amos each held a handful of cards. Brent looked into his polished brass mirror, combing his hair. He was dressing to go walking out with Lisa. Link Hensler leaned against the first bunk, cleaning his nails with a Bowie knife.

"Howdy, Boss," Amos drawled. He was the first to see Wyatt.

"What's up?" Curly asked.

"I came to let you know there'll be a change in the work we laid out for tomorrow," Wyatt said, catching up an empty chair and turning it around. He straddled the backward chair.

"First off, we're gonna scrub Amos's eyeballs with a toothbrush."

Loud hoots and wild laughter crisscrossed the room.

"That'd be your second job," Amos drawled, a slow grin on his heavy face. "The first one would be catching me."

More laughter.

"Actually," their boss man said, "I've decided to fix up that old line shack south of here. I want Slim and Amos to ride over there and start emptying the stable so we can tear it down. It's about to fall in." His quick eyes surveyed the men before him. No one seemed more than mildly interested.

"I'm going over after breakfast, too." He paused. "I'm thinking I'd like to enlarge the corral, so we'll dig up the posts. I'll show you that when the time comes." He glanced around. "Any questions?"

No answer.

"I'll see you in the morning, then."

He flipped the chair back to its original position and strode into the night to find Ben where he'd left him in the trees. Mounting, he held the beautiful animal to a slow walk, hoping to muffle the sound of his passing.

The night had a half-grown moon that filtered through the trees like splashes of gold on black velvet. He let the horse have his head for a short time, knowing that Ben's night sight was better than his own. Once a small branch smacked his head, almost knocking off his flat-crowned hat.

The line shack loomed up, eerily speckled and shadowed with moonlight. He skirted the small clearing that served as a front yard to leave Ben fifty yards away, beyond sight and sound of the house. Stepping from the leather, he wrapped the reins around a branch without tying them. The tension alone would keep the well-trained animal from moving.

Wyatt paused long enough to dig his Peacemaker Colt and gunbelt from the saddlebag and buckle them on. He hadn't wanted to frighten Susan by wearing them, but common sense told him that he'd need a weapon when dealing with a desperate outlaw.

Edging back the way he'd come, Wyatt found a small dry ditch and followed it to the appointed meeting place, a stand of young aspen across from the front door. Soft-footing across leaves and twigs, the sound of his movements seemed like the arrival of a freight train to his tense mind.

At the edge of the copse he whispered, "Banjo? You here?"

"In the flesh," the coarse voice answered. "I been here an hour already."

Wyatt sidled between the saplings and squatted beside the broad shadow that was Banjo. The thin strip of blackness beside the grizzled jaw was his Sharps .56, a wide-bored buffalo gun with a roar like a cannon.

"I laid out the bait real thick," Hammond said. "Told 'em we're gonna tear down the stable and dig up the corral posts. If one of 'em knows the box is buried around here, he'll be almighty anxious to get it out."

Wyatt moved ten feet further toward the cabin and hunkered down on some wet leaves, ears alert, eyes adjusting to the darkness. Half an hour later, he felt the urge to close his eyes. He rubbed his face, fighting sleep, and kept watching.

A few moments later, hoofbeats from the north brought him to full alertness. A horse and rider broke into the clearing and disappeared around the back of the house. Keeping to the trees, the stalkers moved around, carefully placing each foot to avoid a rustling leaf or stick.

Wyatt knew that Banjo was circling in the opposite direction to catch the crook between them. He lifted his shooting iron from its holster and gently replaced it to have it loose and ready. Drawing in a chestful of air, he slowly released it, demanding steadiness from his high-strung hands. Somewhere west of them, an owl demanded, "Who-o-o-o? . . . Who-o-o-o?"

The lanky rancher paused in the shadows at the edge of the corral. Their quarry must have time to find the evidence and condemn himself. He heard scuffling noises inside the stable, then the groaning stable door opened. A feeble lantern glowed next to a pair of legs and the handle of a shovel.

The faceless man didn't hesitate. He strode to a back corner of the corral next to the stable wall and set the lantern on the ground. A dozen thrusts of the shovel and he cast the tool aside. Kneeling, he stretched downward.

"Hold it right there!" Banjo barked. "I don't want to trim your ears, but I will if you move."

Cold steel felt clammy in Wyatt's hand. With nerves taut as a bowstring, he edged around the fence line. Intent on the prey, he stepped through a moonbeam.

With a quick, swift lunge, the outlaw rolled and kicked the lantern to kill the light. In the same instant he fired. Wyatt reacted by instinct rather than design. He felt the Colt buck in his hand and a fiery pain stab his biceps.

From the black depths of the corral came a gasp and soft thud.

Was the man hit? Was he conscious? Was he still armed?

Wyatt swallowed the fear and pain that washed over him. His arm felt warm and sticky from shoulder to elbow. Holstering his gun, he fumbled for his kerchief to staunch the bleeding, thinking, *Won't Susan be in a flap when she gets an eyeful of this!*

A low moan crossed the night air. Was it real or a trick to get the hunters to show themselves?

Wyatt gritted his teeth. *This is a pretty pickle,* he told himself.

A different sort of owl gave a low hoot. Wyatt crept along, knees bent, toward the sound. That night bird wore a ragged Stetson and packed a Sharps.

Wyatt almost bumped into the old-timer before he saw him. "What'll we do now?" he whispered. "He may be layin' for us in there, playin' possum."

"We need some light," Banjo said, stating the obvious.

"Let's set fire to the stable," Wyatt suggested. "It's about to fall in anyway. That'll give us enough light to see him plain as day. A lantern will only draw his fire and likely kill one of us.

"I'm hit," Wyatt added, as an afterthought. "He nicked my arm." Weakness and nausea washed over him. "Go ahead and fire the place, Banjo. We just had a good rain, so the grass won't go. Let's get this show over with." He eased into a sitting position on the ground, head hanging low.

Banjo disappeared inside the stable. He was back in three minutes.

"I put a match to some straw up next to the wall on that side," he whispered. "Everything inside's dry tinder. It won't be long."

A brief flicker grew into a glow then a gleam of orange and yellow light. Acrid smoke pricked their senses.

From the shadows, Banjo and Wyatt watched the corral light up before them. Next to the freshly dug hole lay a prone figure, gun arm outstretched. A pepperbox revolver lay two feet from lifeless fingers. Nimble for his years, Banjo skipped over the fence to retrieve the gun. Wyatt climbed across the boards to reach the scene as Banjo grasped the unconscious man's chin and brought his face into view.

Link Hensler.

A sticky red smear half covered his bald spot. Bending over him, Banjo examined the wound.

"Looks like you creased his scalp," he decided. "He'll probably come around after awhile." Gripping the man's right wrist, he held it toward the light. A jagged, bumpy scar crossed the back of his hand.

Banjo straightened and pulled a wad of rawhide string from his pocket. "We'd best tie him tight. This hombre can make a powerful lot of trouble for us when he wakes up." Working over him like a rodeo contestant on a calf, he bound Hensler's hands in front of his belt buckle.

The stable was blazing beautifully now. Shooting flames rose thirty feet in the air. Inside, a timber crashed to the ground, shaking the earth.

Hensler moaned and turned his head. His eyelids blinked

sleepily. Bleary eyes focused on the men above him. Both Banjo and Wyatt backed out of range of the wounded man's boots.

"Give it up, Hensler," Banjo advised. "You'll only hurt yourself more if you try anything. Wyatt, here, is gonna hold his hogleg ready. If you give me any guff, he'll nail you."

Stark hatred twisting his features, Hensler didn't move. His slack lips spouted words he hadn't learned in Sunday school.

"On your feet now," Banjo commanded. "If you need help, I'll give you a hand." He glanced at Wyatt. "Don't give him an inch, son. He'll kick both of us into next week if he sees a weak spot."

Hensler rolled over to a hands-and-knees position and slowly pulled his feet under him. Panting, he rested his forehead on the ground for a count of ten. Finally, he got erect, weaving slightly. Banjo came behind him and placed strong hands on the wounded man's shoulders.

"Let's find your horse, young fellow. I'll help you mount up."

"Where to now?" Wyatt asked. "We need to get him into town."

"And you need to see Doc Leatherwood," Banjo added. "Let's fetch your buckboard. I'll drive it for you."

The house was dark when they returned to the ranch. While they hitched two buckskins to the buckboard and transferred Hensler to the wagon's back, Wyatt debated whether to wake Susan or not. He finally decided to let her sleep. He was leading the horses across the yard when the front door burst open and Susan, in a dark robe, came running toward them with a glowing lantern swinging from her hand.

"Wyatt! Are you okay?" She grasped his arm and recoiled in the same move. "You're bleeding!"

"It's just a scratch, Susan. Nothing to fret about."

She looked over Wyatt's head. "What's that orange glow in the sky? I woke up and smelled smoke. Then I saw the light above the trees and it frightened me."

"We set fire to the stable behind that old line shack east of here. It's okay. I woke up Slim and Amos so they can make sure it doesn't travel. Banjo and I are on our way into Juniper to turn Hensler over to the sheriff."

"Hensler!" Susan's blue eyes widened. Lifting the light above her head, she peered over the side of the wagon at the bound man lying in back. As an added precaution, Banjo had roped the outlaw's feet to the side post of the wagon. Her eyes narrowed. "To think of all the times he's eaten our food and taken advantage of our hospitality!"

Holding the light to advantage, she inspected Wyatt's arm. "You sure you're okay?"

"I'm fine. When we get to Juniper I'll get Doc Leather-wood to look at it. The sooner we get goin', the sooner I'll be back." He looked at the moon. "At this rate it'll be dawn before you see me again." He stooped to kiss her. "Go back to bed and don't worry."

"You may as well tell a meadowlark not to fly." She squeezed his hand and released it. "Take care of him, Banjo," she called to the still form waiting on the buckboard seat. Banjo's Kelsey and Hensler's buckskin stood tied to the back of the wagon.

"I'll make him behave, Miss Susan," the veteran called. "Good night to you."

Wyatt watched his wife enter their home before he weakly climbed aboard. "Don't waste no time getting there, Banjo," he said. "It's been a long night."

fifteen

Five minutes of pounding brought Dr. Leatherwood to his door. His thick face and broken nose looked sinister in the wee hours.

"What is it?" he asked, holding the door wide and staring into the darkness outside the door.

Banjo prodded Hensler inside. "There's been some gunplay. This man," he pointed to the hostler staggering before him, "robbed the stage." Quickly he told of the evening's events. "If you'll look after the wounds," he finished, "I'll round up Sheriff Feiklin."

The doctor grunted. His bare head reflected the light of the coal oil lamp. "The sheriff won't be in a good mood at this time of night." He turned to Wyatt. "You got a gun?" At Hammond's nod, he said, "Lay it on the table where I can reach it. Hensler, sit in that chair. I'm going to look at Hammond's arm first. Then I'll take care of you."

Leaving the doctor to his business, Banjo stepped into Oak Street, a residential lane running parallel to Main. He traced his way to the end of the dusty road where Feiklin's house lay a stone's throw behind the sheriff's office on Main Street.

Halfway there, he stopped in the middle of the road to take off his hat and rub sleep-hungry eyes with his shirtsleeve. Now that the pressure was off, he suddenly felt exhausted.

A lamp sprang to life seconds after Banjo's knock.

Feiklin's wide jowls jutted through the doorway. He growled, "Can't it wait till morning?"

145

"Sorry, Sheriff," Banjo said, hat in hand, "but we've brought in the thief who robbed the Cedar Grove stage. He got his head creased when we took him. Doc Leatherwood's tendin' to him."

Immediately interested, Feiklin straightened. "You don't say. Give me two shakes to fetch my hat." He disappeared. Banjo stepped away from the door. The sheriff was beside him in minutes. Side by side they strode down the street. "Where'd you catch him?" Feiklin demanded. "We found the cave where he's been hiding, but we missed him. He'd lit a shuck for parts unknown."

"He's not Chance." Banjo's words came out low, distinct, and definite. "He's Link Hensler."

"Hold on!" The lawman stopped short. "You leadin' me on a wild-goose chase?"

"Hensler rubbed burnt cork on his face and hands. He wore a black wig so folks would think him a black man. He found a tall bay horse somewhere and painted a blaze on it to look like Chance's horse."

"A tall bay?" Feiklin demanded. "I keep a bay at the livery stable." His eyes burned with indignation. "You think he used my horse to pull off the robbery?"

"Where else would he find a horse the right size and coloring? There's no doubt he buried the strongbox and rode to the Rocking H to make his trail end there. How could he know where the money was hid except that he hid it? When he thought Wyatt Hammond was gonna dig up that old corral, Hensler made tracks right to the spot and commenced to diggin'." The old cowpoke stepped into a patch of moonlight and stood still, unrelenting eyes on the man at his side. Banjo pushed on. "Why didn't he wear a mask during the holdup?"

Feiklin didn't answer.

"I'll tell you," the old-timer grated out. "He was already wearing one. His black face was a mask. Hammond and I found the makin's of his costume. It's in the buckboard now. Hensler shot Wyatt in the shoulder and got a furrow in his own skull for his trouble."

He paused to draw in a breath. "You had your mind made up from the time you heard about the color of the man's skin. If you'd checked further, you'd have learned that the thief had skin the color of coal. He couldn't have been Chance, Feiklin. Not in a hundred years."

The big man didn't say more, but his curt attitude simmered way down. When they stepped through the doctor's door, Leatherwood was putting a final layer of cloth over Hensler's pate. The wounded man looked as if he wore a white cotton nightcap. On the sofa sat Wyatt with his arm in a sling, the Colt gripped in his uninjured hand.

"Howdy, Sheriff," Wyatt called. "Welcome to the party."

"I hear you fellows had some excitement," Feiklin drawled. His voice practically echoed in the small room. "Hensler, what do you have to say for yourself?"

"Nothin'." The guilty man stared at the floor. "I'm gettin' me a lawyer before I say a word."

"You'll have a while to wait then," the sheriff said. "The circuit judge isn't due for two months. I suppose we'll ship you to Denver. The big boys can take care of you."

He turned to Wyatt and Banjo. "I guess you boys can split the reward money. I'll write up a promissory note. You can cash it at the bank."

"We'll pick it up later, Sheriff," Wyatt told him. "At the moment home means more to me than any amount of money." As an afterthought he added, "We'll tie Hensler's horse to the doc's hitching rail. You can get him later."

"Let's go," Feiklin said to the guilty man. He glanced at Banjo. "I'll return your rawhide later. This turkey had best stay trussed." Drawing his six-shooter, he marched Hensler outside.

"Thanks, Doc," Wyatt said, standing. "We'll leave you to pound your pillow. There's a whole hour till dawn."

"I slept through the night at least five times last month," the doctor said, grinning wearily. "Seems like every baby within thirty miles wants to get introduced to the world by candlelight."

Firm knuckles outside the door brought concern to the good man's face. Breaking away from the conversation, he pulled up the latch.

"Can you come, Doc?" Steve's white face appeared in the doorway. "Megan's gonna have that baby tonight."

"I'll be right there." Leatherwood grabbed his coat from the tree by the door and scooped his black bag from the table. "Sorry, gentlemen. We'll have to make it a short good-bye."

"Banjo!" Steve exclaimed. "What brings you here?"

"We brought in Hensler. He held up the stage and framed Chance. He shot Wyatt's arm, so we stopped in to see the Doc."

The nervous father interrupted Banjo to say to Leatherwood, "I've got the buckboard, Doc. You can ride with me." He held up his hand, palm out, toward his friends. "We'll talk it over later, Banjo. Em's watching over Megan, but I've got to get the Doc there pronto."

Banjo chuckled. "Take it easy, old man. Babies are born every day."

"Not mine!" Steve retorted, rushing away. He clambered into the seat beside the black-coated medical man, released the brake, and slapped the reins. Billy and Star jumped into a brisk trot, trace chains jangling.

Wyatt and Banjo paused on the street in the damp coolness of the morning.

"We'd best let Chance in on the good news," Wyatt said, easing the sling where it bit into his neck. "He can ride home with me in the buckboard."

Banjo stretched widely and ended by swinging his arms back and forth. "I believe I'll wake up, directly." He stepped to a full water barrel at the corner of the doctor's house and splashed his face. His black bandanna acted as a makeshift towel. Kelsey's head was drooping when they reached the buckboard. Banjo gave the faithful donkey a slap on the rump, bringing the animal's head around. "We're almost home, pal." He untied the weary palomino, led him to the water barrel for a drink, and carefully tied him in front of the doctor's house.

Wyatt climbed into the wagon and sank back on the hard bench. "Go ahead and drive, Banjo," he said through tense lips. "This arm's throbbin' like the dickens."

"Hi-yup!" Banjo called, easing off the brake. The gelding set out as if he smelled water. In minutes Juniper faded into the distance behind them.

A faint ochre gleam surged above the dark horizon. It moved upward, becoming an orange strip with a burst of yellow on top. Orange and yellow widened—pushing, pushing the indigo sky until light conquered the night. Gradually, yet somehow suddenly, the sky was azure, and the sun blithely floated free of the land.

Tired as he was, Banjo felt the wonder of a fresh, new day.

The wagon creaked to a halt under the giant tree and Banjo wound the reins around the whipstand.

"I'll wait here," Wyatt said. "You don't need me no how."

Above the lone walker, a flock of honking geese cut a V in

the cloudy sky. A lizard skittered out of the trail, avoiding heavy boots.

Twenty paces up the hill, he paused and cupped hands to his mouth, "Chance! It's me, Banjo! I'm comin' up!" Was the hunted man still in the cave? Feiklin said he'd left. If so, where had he gone? Five more paces and Banjo helloed again. Dry bushes rustled in the mouth of the cave. A bushel-size piece fell away. Relieved, Banjo hurried forward.

Before him stood a shadow, a shell of the person he'd seen twenty-four hours before. Thick dust covered Chance's face and hair. Ground-in dirt stiffened his clothes. Wrinkled and drawn as a man twice his age, his cheeks sank in. The black man's frame seemed almost skeletal.

"Good news!" Banjo announced by way of greeting. "Last night Wyatt and I caught Link Hensler red-handed digging up the strongbox stolen from the stage. He's sweatin' it out in the calaboose right now. You're free. You can go home."

Shock blanked out Chance's expression for an instant before his eyes crinkled in disbelief. "Hensler?" He stepped back to let Banjo enter. "I thought sure Savage was the man."

Again, Banjo told the story. "Wyatt took a bullet in the arm. He's waiting in the buckboard. Doc Leatherwood just patched him up."

Chance raked trembling fingers through his gritty hair. "I've died a hundred hideous deaths since the sheriff came up here yesterday. I'd just about decided I have only two choices: hanging or starving. If I had a six-gun, I might have taken a third way out."

Chance shied away from his visitor's kindly look. How could he face Banjo after he'd doubted the old man's integrity, scoffed at his sincerity?

"You and Mr. Wyatt risked your lives for the likes of me. Why?"

"Can we sit down?" Banjo asked.

They sank to the hard earth. Bottom lip thrust forward, Chance stared at the ground, waiting.

Banjo's rough voice softened to a low pitch. He spoke slowly, choosing his word with care. "You've endured more grief than most men, Chance. I know a small bit of what you feel." He told the story of his wife and son. "I've felt my insides churn with grief so thick, so hard, I thought I'd die. I wished I could die.

"I despised those Injuns. I used to dream of how I'd ride into their camp and get revenge. Hate was eatin' me alive.

"What I'm trying to tell you, Chance, is that I understand. I know what it means to hurt.

"If I can only make it clear." Banjo's lips puckered as he groped for words. "Those men who put your people into slavery, those Kiowas who murdered my Mary, didn't cause that pain because of their skin color. They did it because they were wicked.

"There's still plenty of that brand around, too. I don't have to tell you that. The Good Book says, 'The heart is deceitful above all things and desperately wicked.' That applies to everyone the world over. And folks can't straighten themselves out. The only way a lost man can get straight is in a coffin. Jesus alone can change an evil heart." Chance raised his head and stared at the square of light in the doorway.

Banjo went on, "You were surprised because Wyatt took a bullet to help you. I know someone who went even further. He died a horrible death for you. It was Jesus. He wants to take away your pain. But you must give it to Him. Give Him your pain. Turn loose of your grief. Salvation means a life of joy and peace like you've never imagined.

"It's a gift, Chance. Will you take it?"

The atmosphere thickened with the weight of that question. Chance studied his soil-caked boots, Em's voice echoing in his ears, "A real Christian looks past the color of a man's skin. Jesus died for all of us, you know."

Finally, the haunted man spoke. His voice creaked. "When the posse came into the cave, I crawled into my hole and pulled the stone in after me. One of them walked into the tunnel, looking for me. He took a shovel and dug at the false wall." Chance drew a trembling breath.

"I've never prayed in my life, but I prayed then." He rubbed his face with stiff fingers. "You know what happened? That man quit digging and walked away. Five minutes later, the posse walked out of here and didn't come back." He swallowed hard.

"At that moment, I knew God is real." His voice cracked, but he kept talking. "That was the first time since I left my mama that I really felt someone care for me."

Banjo started to speak, but Chance waved him off.

"You folks cared, too. I see that now, but I didn't believe it then." For the first time, he looked directly at the man sitting beside him. "I can't keep going on like I've been. I want what Em has, what you have."

Banjo placed a calloused hand on Chance's sagging shoulder and closed his eyes, saying, "Let's pray."

❧

Hands up to shade his eyes, Chance stepped into the light of day. He clutched a bundle of blankets and a filthy coat in his arms. With Banjo, he strode across the hillside toward the buckboard where Wyatt lay on the seat, dozing.

At the crunching of boots on gravel, the wounded man sat up and scratched his beard. "I was wonderin' if you-all had decided to camp out a few days longer."

"Sorry to keep you waitin', Wyatt," Banjo called. "We had some things that we needed to talk out."

Wyatt took stock of Chance's appearance. "Howdy, Chance. Looks like you could use a hot tub and a plate full of biscuits and gravy."

Chance nodded and managed a tired smile. "Not in that order, I hope." He threw the blankets into the back of the wagon and climbed in after them. "I could put away a cow and a half about now."

They hit the trail and Banjo let the buckskins have their heads. Sailing breezes whistled through the clothes of the three men. They felt the chill, but it gave them pleasure, quickened their weary blood.

"Would you be free from the burden of sin. . . ." Banjo's music reached far across the rolling hills as they headed toward the mountains.

Stretched out in the back, Chance closed his eyes, savoring the song and the deep peace within him. After he cleaned up and filled his gnawing stomach, he'd sleep for about two weeks. Then he'd pay Emma a visit. He smiled.

"Here's where we part," Banjo announced, pulling up the reins. "Get yourself home, Wyatt, and let Susan fuss over you."

"I'll enjoy every minute of it." Wyatt laughed. "Be seein' you, Banjo. You ever need a job, look me up."

The grizzled cowpoke chuckled. "I'll do that."

He swung his legs over the side of the buckboard, pausing to say, "We'll get together for some Bible study, Chance, once you rest up. I'll be over to see you."

Chance climbed into Banjo's seat and lifted the straps of leather. New light glimmered in his eyes as he said, "God bless you, Banjo. I thank you."

"Thank the Lord, my brother," Banjo responded warmly. "He's the One who should get the praise."

Wyatt heard their conversation with growing interest, a puzzled wrinkle to his brow. Banjo trod back to untie Kelsey and step into the saddle.

Noting Wyatt's expression, Chance told him, "I found Jesus today, Mr. Wyatt. Have you ever met Him?"

Kelsey turned down the trail toward home. When Banjo looked back, the buckboard had lurched ahead with Chance and Wyatt in serious conversation.

The Circle C seemed quiet when Banjo arrived. Something about the scent of woodsmoke from his own chimney gave him a glad, satisfied feeling. Leading the tired donkey into his stall, Banjo saw to the animal's needs and headed through the stable's back door to the spring behind the house. He paused long enough for an icy drink from the tin cup hanging from a rawhide cord before opening the kitchen door.

At the stove Em fried eggs, a plate of steaming steaks on the counter beside her.

"Dish me up half a dozen of them steaks," Banjo ordered, his twinkle showing, "and a dozen eggs."

Em's head jerked around, her eyes wide. "Where you been, Banjo? We'se all wonderin' what become of you."

"Well, first off, me and Wyatt caught us a holdup man named Link Hensler. As I speak, your friend Chance is on his way home."

Em raised her face toward heaven, eyes closed. "The Lord be praised," she breathed. Her round eyes were moist when she opened them, and she wore a brand-new smile. "Well, come on in and have a seat. Things have been happenin' here, too. Looks like nobody in this family got any sleep last night. Except'n Jeremy, that is!"

"How's Megan?"

"Sleepin' like the baby beside her," Em announced happily. "The most beautiful little girl you ever laid your eyes on, Banjo.

"Mr. Steve's snoozin', too, but he said to wake him up when breakfast is ready."

Jeremy burst in the front door. A brown smudge already colored his nose. "Did you catch him, Banjo?" he demanded, claiming the seat next to his hero.

"Sure did." He ran through the much-told tale yet another time. "The Doc bound up Wyatt's arm. It's not serious, but it's givin' him some double-distilled pain at the moment."

Em set two plates on the table. "I'm startin' you out with two steaks and four eggs, Banjo. The biscuits will be ready in two minutes." She chuckled. "If you want more, just holler." She headed toward the bedroom door. "I'll fetch Mr. Steve."

In a moment she returned with Steve two paces behind her. Thick stubble coated his jaw, and his eyes were bloodshot. He paused outside the bedroom door to massage his face.

Banjo jumped to his feet to shake the weary man's hand. "Congratulations, Chamberlin!"

Fatigue forgotten, Steve's grin split his face. "I'm a rich man, Banjo. Richer than Vanderbilt." He sank into the chair at the end of the table and watched Em lay a plate in front of him.

"Em!" A call came from the bedroom. Em hurried to Megan's side and closed the door.

"How's Chance?" Steve asked, attacking the steak.

"Headed for home. He received the Lord this mornin'. I didn't tell Em. I reckon, it's his news to tell her with what's taken place between them."

The events of last night provided much conversation with

Jeremy, jaws in motion, hanging on every word. They lingered over second cups of coffee, relaxing tired muscles and weary minds.

"Want to see the baby, Banjo?" Em asked, appearing in the bedroom doorway. "Megan says you can come in now."

"Does a chicken have lips?" the cowhand retorted with a smile.

Jeremy slipped a small hand into Banjo's wide, hard palm. They approached the room with quiet reverence, Jeremy's eyes as big as teacups.

Under the wedding-ring quilt lay Megan with her hair cascading over the pillow. A peaceful glow surrounded her weary face.

Smiling softly, she said, "Come and see what I've got, Jeremy." Near the side of the bed, she held a closely wrapped bundle in the crook of her arm. Jeremy peeked over the edge of the white flannel blanket, intensely curious yet awed. He froze, cast an incredulous look at Megan's face, and leaned forward for closer inspection.

Tiny fists grasped the blanket's border. Snuggled against her mama's safe warm side lay a ruddy munchkin face crowned with curling black hair. Still grasping Banjo's hand, Jeremy stretched forth a finger to stroke the tiny cheek.

"When she wakes up, you can hold her," the new mother promised the little boy.

"Congratulations, Miss Megan," Banjo breathed. He glanced at Steve, hovering at the end of the bed. "You're right, Chamberlin. You're a mighty rich man."

Steve looked at his wife and a wide soft arc of joy and love passed between them.

Jeremy wiggled an index finger under the baby's hand. The movement caught Megan's eyes.

"Her name is Katie," she told him. "After Mother."

Jeremy burst out, "When can she play with me? Will she be able to catch a ball?"

They stayed three minutes more, answering Jeremy's questions, listening to his observations, until Banjo tugged at the boy's hand.

"We'd best let Miss Megan rest, Jem," he said. "She was up most of the night, and she's awful tired."

Jeremy looked at his sister for confirmation.

Megan nodded. "You can help Em give Katie a bath later, honey. There'll be lots of time to play with the baby."

From that point on, the Chamberlin household took on certain aspects of heaven: relief, rejoicing. . .and no night there. Little Katie loved the midnight watches. Unless hunger was the problem, Em sat up with the baby to let the exhausted young mother sleep. Normal routine blew to the four winds and Em lost complete track of time.

sixteen

The morning Chance rode in, he found Em sweeping the porch. Broom in hand, she stared dumbly at his approaching horse, wondering, *What day of the week is it? Saturday?*

Megan and the baby slept. Jeremy had ridden into the woods with Banjo and Steve to collect yet more firewood. Em propped the broom against the house and waited on the top step. Now that Chance had come, she was anxious to hear his version of his fearful escapade. She noticed that he still looked thin, though not nearly as haggard as before.

Chance dropped Po'boy's reins and strode toward her, his face alight. Em observed his long stride, the tilt of his head, his keen eyes.

Something's changed, she thought. *Would having his name cleared make him look like that?*

"Good morning, Emma!" Even his voice had a different ring.

Em smiled widely. "Is it mornin'? That new little girl has kept me a-goin' so much, I don't know which end's up." She put out her hand. "I'se mighty glad to see you, Chance. How are you?"

"I've never been better." He squeezed her fingers and didn't let go. "Do you feel like walking?"

"The fresh air will do me good, I reckon." She stepped down to his level, and they headed toward the stable and beyond.

"Banjo told me what happened to you. . .about Sheriff

Feiklin comin' to the cave and all." She shuddered. "I'm mighty glad it's all over."

Chance chuckled. "Miss Susan about smothered me when I got home. She fed me steak and beans until I couldn't hold another bite. While I stuffed myself, she heated about ten gallons of water so I could take a bath while Slim buried my clothes. Since then, she's only let me sleep and eat. Tomorrow I start cooking again."

He changed the subject when they had crossed the stream. "How's the new mother getting along?"

In few words Em listed the goings-on of the past four days. "Megan and the baby are right as rain. God has been so good to us."

"He sure has," Chance agreed, his voice strangely quiet.

Em stared at him. "Something about you has changed. I knew it the first I laid eyes on you, Chance. What's happened?"

He smiled and a soft light turned on within him. "I found Jesus, Emma. Or maybe I should say He found me. Banjo talked with me in the cave, the morning he and Mr. Wyatt brought in Hensler.

"It was amazing how it all took place. You see, God already had my attention." He told her of the man digging into the false wall.

"So when Banjo laid it out for me clear and plain, I knew I had to surrender." He laughed softly. "When God's got you covered, you better come out with your hands up."

"Praise be to Jesus!" Em's face took on a glory light of its own. "You don't know how many nights I laid awake prayin' for you."

"Banjo called on me yesterday," his deep voice continued. "He brought his new Bible. We're reading through the Gospel of John together." He stooped to pick up a large pinecone and toss it into the stream. "I'm going to get me a Bible, Emma, if I have to pay two hundred dollars and ride two hundred miles."

She clapped her hands together. "Wouldn't it be passin' wonderful to hear you a-readin' it!"

Chance grasped her arm and stopped their progress. They stood among the pines at the bottom edge of the empty cornfield.

"Emma, can I make you change your mind about marrying me?" He took a step forward and turned to face her. "Please think it over, Emma. Now that I'm a Christian I see that my dreams have been nothing but an empty shell. Things can never make a person happy. Only God can do that." He stepped closer, speaking softly, gazing into her eyes.

Em stood stock-still. This time she couldn't break the spell, didn't realize it even existed.

The man continued, speaking intensely. "You thought you were coming to Colorado to help Miss Megan, but I believe that God brought you here for me. We both love Jesus. If we love each other as well, the circle's complete." That sad look—the one that first reached out to Em— showed itself again. He stood as though frozen, waiting for the verdict.

His appeal squeezed Em's heart. How could she turn him away?

Tears spilled over. "Yes, Chance," she whispered. "I will marry you."

In an instant he folded her into the safe shelter of his arms. Em squeezed her brimming eyes tight and knew that this is where she was meant to be.

They stood together for a moment before he released her and caught her hand. She stuffed her damp handkerchief into the pocket of her work dress. Without making a conscious decision, they veered toward the lake. An irate squirrel chattered from a pine bough, its cheeks bulging.

They spoke of life and love and the surprising turns that God brings people through.

"The sheriff came yesterday to return my silver nuggets," the man said when they reached the edge of blue water. "He had a slip from the assayer's office saying it's worth $2,750. That ought to be enough to get us started. Next week I'll go to the land office and see what's still open in these parts.

"He also apologized." Chance grimaced. "After a fashion."

Em looked up at him, surprised. "What did he say?"

"He told me he should have done more checking before telling the town it was I that robbed the stage. He said he'll be more careful in the future."

"Well, I guess that's some comfort."

"I wouldn't count Feiklin a heartfelt friend, but at least he was man enough to say what he did." They walked in the mottled shade near the water. A fish splashed on the surface and disappeared. A woodpecker's tattoo echoed through the mountains.

"How about a Christmas wedding, Emma, if we can find a preacher? With some help, I can put up a small log cabin in a few days. We'll add on a room or two as time goes by. Wouldn't it be grand to snuggle in together and wait out the winter?"

As though waking from deep sleep, Em exclaimed, "Oh! What am I gonna do about Jeremy? It was him that played those tricks on you, Chance. He was scared you'd take me away." The handkerchief reappeared. "Now it looks like the boy was right."

"Would Miss Megan let him stay with us?" Chance asked. "Jeremy's a fine boy. I know we could be friends."

"I'd have to talk to Miss Megan. I don't know how she'd feel about that."

"Would it help if I talk to him?" he asked.

"Maybe." She shrugged. "I've been prayin' about it, Chance. But so far, I don't have no answers."

Perched close together on a flat rock, they talked and planned for another hour.

"I've been thinking, Emma. When a man marries, his wife takes his name." He looked at her, an amused expression on his features. "I seem to be lacking something essential there."

"That don't. . ." Em began, but he cut her off.

"What do you think of taking *Calahan* for our last name? Banjo's my father in the Lord. I think it would be fitting."

"That's a wonderful thought! I'd like to be with you when you tell Banjo." She laughed. "I can see his expression now."

With much regret they retraced the path toward the house. The sun beamed on them from high above.

"I'd best go to Miss Megan," Em said when they reached the porch steps.

"You think she'd let me see the baby?"

"Why, sure! I'd have asked you myself if I thought you'd want to." She climbed the stairs and opened the door, Chance close behind her. "Let me see if they'se still sleepin'."

Megan was sitting up when Em peeked inside. The baby lay on the bed, waving little hands.

The lean woman stepped through the door. "Is it okay if I take Katie out so Chance can see her?"

Two minutes later, holding the wiggling bundle in tender arms, Em joined Chance on the sofa.

"Her name's *Katie* after Miss Megan's dear mama." Em smiled into the wide blue eyes, so serious. She looked up to her guest. "Would you like to hold her?"

Grinning, Chance reached for the flannel parcel. He gently cradled the tiny girl, touched her hair and her hands. She stared into his eyes with the wise expression known only to newborns.

"What do you know?" he exclaimed in muted tones. "My first granddaughter. Who would have guessed she would be a white child?" He laughed, an infectious sound. Em laughed, too, her heart so full she had to keep dabbing her eyes.

The mantel clock had passed noon before he said good-bye and rode away. Carrying Katie back to her mama, Em entered the bedroom.

Wearing a soft blue gown, Megan sat on the edge of the bed. By doctor's orders, she wasn't allowed to get up for ten days. Em laid the sweet bundle on the bed.

"What happened, Em?" Megan asked. "You look like the cat who swallowed the canary."

"He received the Lord, Miss Megan. We'se gettin' married." She paused. "It would have broke my heart to turn him down again. I couldn't say no."

"I thought so!" Radiating happiness, Megan held her arms out for a hug. "I'm so glad for you." She squeezed Em hard.

Em clung to her. "I don't want to leave you, Miss Megan. Or Jeremy. I feel like I'm being cut in two." She straightened. "Chance needs me. But so does Jeremy. How can I tell the child?"

Megan stared at the floor, considering. Baby Katie let out a wee cry. "Don't tell Jeremy yet, Em," she said, reaching for her daughter. "Let's pray about this awhile."

Prayer was about all Em accomplished through the next

two weeks. Her emotions ran up and down so quickly, most of the time she didn't know whether to laugh or cry.

Chance appeared at odd times, whenever he could spare a couple of hours from his duties. His warm looks and broad smiles made it no secret that he was as much in love as a boy of eighteen. Whenever he appeared, Megan and Steve shared a secret smile, but Jeremy's countenance resembled a thundercloud.

A few days later, Chance arrived to find the boy sitting on the top step of the porch, his determined hands gripping a piece of pine and his new knife. As always, Lobo hovered nearby. Chance had become such a regular guest, the dog merely sniffed his cuffs.

Jeremy gave an up-from-under glance at the man, expecting him to pass by. This time, however, Chance sat on the step beside the child.

Jeremy's chin sank lower. He continued scraping at the wood, sending irregular chips to the floor. The pine resembled a half-eaten ear of corn.

"What are you making?" Chance asked, hoping to break the ice.

The answer was barely audible. "A dog." Shrinking away, he scored the lump of wood with vengeance.

Chance saw that the only way to begin his speech was to begin it. He plunged ahead. "Jeremy, I want to tell you that I don't plan to separate you from Em. I know you love her. She loves you, too."

Jeremy's hands became still. He stared at his handiwork.

The adult rubbed nervous hands on his pant legs. "I'm going to buy property as close to the Circle C as I can." He hesitated, then rushed ahead. "Em and I are going to get married and live there. We want you to be with us, Jeremy. You can visit often or even come to live with us, if Miss Megan will let you." Chance was running out of ammunition and he wasn't sure if the battle was over yet.

"You're a great lad, Jeremy. If I'd had a boy of my own, I would have wanted him to be like you. I wish we could be friends."

The towheaded child turned toward him. "Do you know how to fish?"

Taken aback, Chance replied, "Why sure. It's one of my favorite ways to pass an afternoon."

"Banjo and Steve don't take to fishin', and I wish I could learn how."

"Would you like to go tomorrow? After lunch?"

The dark look disappeared. In its place came a cautious acceptance, a tentative approval. "Okay," he said quietly.

"We may not get much fishing done the first day," Chance told him, relaxing a little. "We'll have to find some good poles and fix a line. I have some hooks. I made them myself." He gave Lobo a friendly pat. "We'll go at the warmest part of the day. To the lake. Okay?"

"Maybe Em'll pack us some sandwiches," the boy added, hopefully.

Chance chuckled. "I'm sure she will. She thinks I'm about to fade away from starvation these days." He stood up. "I'll see you tomorrow, then," he said.

Jeremy's knife gouged at the figure, sending a chunk to the floor.

☙

Megan sat with Em in the living room the next afternoon while Chance and Jeremy were on their fishing expedition. The boy had been too excited to eat lunch. Em wrapped sandwiches and placed them in a tin to carry along. She shared a secret smile with Chance before the twosome set off.

Megan sat on the sofa, folding diapers, while Em bounced Katie on her knee. "Have Chance come for supper Friday night," Megan suggested. "That will be November first."

"He's planning on comin' over then anyways, Miss Megan." She broke off to make some absurd clicking noises into the baby's face and was rewarded with Katie's studious expression.

Em looked at Megan to ask, "What do you want to have for supper that night?"

"Barbecued steaks and baked potatoes. Wyatt and Susan will be coming, too."

"You sure you aren't oversteppin'?" Em asked, eyebrows raised. "You still ain't too strong."

"I'll be fine. Just invite Chance for the meal when he and Jeremy get back." She picked up a wrinkled diaper and snapped it loudly.

Friday evening, Chance rode in alongside the Rocking H buckboard. Susan wore a long black coat with a large stiff bonnet against the cold night air. After they stepped down, Banjo helped Wyatt unhitch the horse, Jeremy following every move.

Susan carried a large basket into the house. She set it on the kitchen counter. "Don't touch that, Em," she said. "I'll take care of it later."

Em bent over the oven, basting the steaks. "Okay, Miss Susan," she said, straightening. She inspected the cloth-covered wicker, her curiosity piqued. *What's goin' on?* she wondered.

Chance stood inside the door, hat in hand. As a guest, he didn't feel he should join Em in the kitchen, yet he didn't want to stay far away from her in the sitting room, either. Em noticed his predicament and called, "Come talk to me while I finish, Chance."

Relieved, he slipped his hat on a peg and strode to her side. In a moment, he laughed when she dropped a piece of meat on the open oven door. He grabbed a fork to help her retrieve it.

Jeremy skipped through the back door and straight to the man in Em's kitchen. "Look at this, Chance," he chirped, holding out a stick. "Should I notch it here to hold the string? See where I trimmed down the end? I wanted to make a better rod for the next time we go to the lake."

Dropping the steak to its platter, Chance straightened up to regard the boy's masterpiece. He picked it up for a better look. "Nice job, Son. If you notch it here," he pointed, "the string will grip good and tight."

Jeremy took the rod and, pulling his knife from his overalls pocket, headed for the porch steps.

Baby in arms, Megan entered the living room.

"How's the new mother?" Susan asked, approaching Megan. "Mind if I hold her?"

Megan relinquished her burden and found a seat on the sofa. "I'm starting to feel like myself again, thank the Lord."

"We had some startling news this morning," Susan said, choosing a perch on the chair. She laid Katie on her knees, both hands cupped under the tiny head—the best position for a chat.

"What's happened?" Megan asked.

"Brent and Lisa eloped last night. He left a note for Amos. Amos brought it to Wyatt this morning."

Megan's face drew into a frown. "Will they come back to Juniper? What about his job?"

"Your guess beats mine," Susan replied, sadly. "The Feiklin family has a lion's share of heartaches today. I guess everyone does at one time or another." Turning to the sweet bundle on her lap, she cooed, "Hello, little lady."

Wyatt stepped through the front door and drew up short. "Careful, Susan," he warned. "I hear that womenfolk catch a strange fever from holding a tiny bundle like that."

Entering behind him, Banjo chuckled. "That's a fact, Hammond. I've seen it happen."

"You men go chase your cows or something," Susan retorted. "Let me have some peace." She smiled down at the infant.

At the meal, Megan seated wondering Em with Chance at the head of the table. Steve remained standing when everyone had found a chair.

"We're gathered together today to honor a special couple who are about to enter the blessed state of marriage."

Embarrassed, Chance and Em shared a startled glance. Em's eyes widened as she stared at Megan's wide smile. Jeremy beamed along with everyone else.

Steve continued his speech. "We want you, Chance and Em, to know that we wish you a long and happy life together and to pledge our help as neighbors whenever you may need us." He bowed his head saying, "Let's ask God to bless this new family."

His heartfelt prayer touched Chance like nothing else could. Under the table he squeezed Em's hand.

After the food disappeared, Susan fetched the mystery basket from the kitchen. She laid aside the towel covering and drew out a white sheet cake.

"No wonder you chased me out of the kitchen this morning," Chance said, laughter in his voice.

As Susan picked up a knife to cut the cake, Steve half rose to thrust a folded paper at Chance.

Em peered over her intended's shoulder at the maze of lines and letters drawn on it.

"It's a surveyor's map," Chance told her. He looked at Steve. "What's this?"

"See the red plot beside the lake?" Steve asked. "That's yours. A wedding present from Megan and I. Forty acres of grazing or farmland opening on the water."

Astonished, Chance stared at Steve, then pored over the map. He looked up. "I'm not sure I should take this," he stammered.

"It's a selfish gift," Steve added quickly. "We wanted to keep Em close enough for Jeremy to visit her every day. Please take it, Chance. I've already got my lawyer drawing up the deed."

Wyatt leaned over to pull a small sack from under his chair. "This is from Banjo and I," he said, handing the clinking leather pouch to Chance. "It's the reward money for catching Hensler."

"Use it to stake you through the winter," Banjo added. "You'll need feed for your horse and all."

Chance balanced the money in his palm. He swallowed the lump rising below his Adam's apple. "There's no way to thank you all," he managed.

"Be happy," Megan said, eyes shining. "That's the very best way to thank us."

"Would you mind if we eat that cake later?" Chance asked Susan. "We've got an hour till dark, and I'd like to see the land." He squeezed Em's hand. "Want to come?"

"Does a chicken have lips?" she replied, drawing a chuckle from Banjo.

Taking down her wool shawl, she followed her man outside.

"If we step smartly, we can walk over," he said. He slipped a firm arm about her waist. "Emma, my love, let's take a look at the home place."

A Letter To Our Readers

Dear Reader:

In order that we might better contribute to your reading enjoyment, we would appreciate your taking a few minutes to respond to the following questions. When completed, please return to the following:

Rebecca Germany, Managing Editor
Heartsong Presents
PO Box 719
Uhrichsville, Ohio 44683

1. Did you enjoy reading *Changes of the Heart*?
   ☐ Very much. I would like to see more books
      by this author!
   ☐ Moderately
      I would have enjoyed it more if _____

   _____

2. Are you a member of **Heartsong Presents**? ☐ Yes ☐ No
   If no, where did you purchase this book?_____

   _____

3. What influenced your decision to purchase this
   book? (Check those that apply.)

   ☐ Cover   ☐ Back cover copy

   ☐ Title   ☐ Friends

   ☐ Publicity   ☐ Other_____

4. How would you rate, on a scale from 1 (poor) to 5
   (superior), the cover design?_____

5. On a scale from 1 (poor) to 10 (superior), please rate the following elements.

___Heroine   ___Plot

___Hero   ___Inspirational theme

___Setting   ___Secondary characters

6. What settings would you like to see covered in **Heartsong Presents** books?_____

_____

_____

7. What are some inspirational themes you would like to see treated in future books?_____

_____

_____

8. Would you be interested in reading other **Heartsong Presents** titles? ❏ Yes   ❏ No

9. Please check your age range:
   ❏ Under 18   ❏ 18-24   ❏ 25-34
   ❏ 35-45   ❏ 46-55   ❏ Over 55

10. How many hours per week do you read? _____

Name _____

Occupation_____

Address_____

City_____State_____Zip_____

Only You

*A Romantic Collection
of Inspirational Novellas*

Valentine's Day—a day of love, romance, and dreams. *Only You,* a collection of four all-new contemporary novellas from **Heartsong Presents** authors, will be available in January 1998. What better way to celebrate than with this collection written especially for Valentine's Day. Authors Sally Laity, Loree Lough, Debra White Smith, and Kathleen Yapp have practically become household names to legions of romance readers and this collection includes their photos and biographies.

(352 pages, Paperbound, 5" x 8")

......Hearts♥ng ......

HEARTSONG PRESENTS TITLES AVAILABLE NOW:

·········· Presents ··········

Great Inspirational Romance at a Great Price!

Heartsong Presents books are inspirational romances in contemporary and historical settings, designed to give you an enjoyable, spirit-lifting reading experience. You can choose wonderfully written titles from some of today's best authors like Peggy Darty, Sally Laity, Tracie Peterson, Colleen L. Reece, Lauraine Snelling, and many others.

When ordering quantities less than twelve, above titles are $2.95 each.
Not all titles may be available at time of order.